Crossed

Bernette Sherman

Mount Hope Media, LLC

Copyright © 2018, 2022 2026 by Bernette Sherman

Original Copyright © 2016 A. Bernette

All rights reserved.

No portion of this book may be reproduced or used, by human or artificial intelligence, in any form without written permission from the publisher or author, except as permitted by U.S. copyright law.

Published by Mount Hope Media, LLC Atlanta, GA

ISBN-13: 978-0692721056 (Original Paperback)

ISBN-10: 0692721053 (Original Paperback)

https://www.MountHopeMedia.com

https://BernetteSherman.com

DEDICATION

Dedicated to those who understand that Karma is ever-flowing, ever seeking the balance the law requires.
A special dedication to my husband, my children, and my mother.

Contents

1. About Karma 1
2. Prologue 3
3. One 5
4. Two 10
5. Three 21
6. Four 26
7. Five 32
8. Six 38
9. Seven 48
10. Eight 55
11. Nine 65
12. Ten 75

13. Eleven 81
14. Twelve 93
15. Thirteen 99
16. Fourteen 104
17. Fifteen 114
18. Sixteen 124
19. Seventeen 130
20. Eighteen 136
21. Nineteen 142
22. Twenty 147
Also by Bernette 155
About the Author 157
23. About the Author 159
24. The Wait (Chapter One) 160
25. Two 166
26. Three 171
27. Four 176

About Karma

From the Author

Life must balance, and while it seeks to restore balance when it is out of alignment, it does not judge; it simply does. For order is the Universe's natural state, and it will always seek to be in order and in balance.

When we recognize this, that Karma is simply the natural outflow of life - actions, thoughts, feelings, words, expression - we realize that we hold a great deal of power over how Karma plays out for our own lives.

It is what it is, doing what it is supposed to do. It doesn't judge our actions or thoughts but rather seeks to keep the balance that allows the order the Universe constantly seeks.

Just as the rainbow comes after the rain and children are born through the struggle of birth, there is order, purpose, and balance sought throughout all of nature.

Now, let's get our karma on.

PROLOGUE

Kaela

FROM ABOVE, I WATCHED it all unfold. Lana Fier was his first case. My new Karma Crusader requires more training and control if he is to follow the directives set out by the unseen force of law, the Universal Karmic Force, one of many universal forces.

I've been doing this a while, but this new human age makes things move differently. Maybe that affected things with him. Them. Cell phones and apps meant they could get information faster than before.

Everything is faster. But this is just the way things go. I share this story because it's how I crossed paths with them. At the time I didn't know what would happen, but now, I can look back and see it happened as it needed to.

What I have always understood as part of the UKF is that every action has a reaction. Whether it is positive or negative, all things must be balanced. I also understand that it's a lot of work. Which is why they assigned me Maxwell to train so I can have help in administering karma. You'll learn how things went in what follows.

I will say, why Raguel thought Maxwell could handle the role still baffles me, but I was not in charge of recruiting. There are qualities that should be sought in any Karma Crusader, especially any on my team.

One

Kaela

The blustery wind blew against her face on that cold and dreary autumn day as she tried to move towards the barely visible structure ahead of her. A strong gust picked up the dry, brittle leaves cast down to the ground and swept them in circles around her. She coughed and choked on their fine dust. The ominous black clouds stirring above her head gave an eerie and desolate feeling.

Then, it was quiet for a fleeting moment before the rain began to fall. First in plops and then hard like sheets, blinding her as it pelted against her worried face. The slanted rain didn't stop the leaves from scattering and then gathering around her, whirling in a circle faster and faster. More and more of the dead brown leaves gathered around her as she struggled to see and break out of their hold.

The barren trees spoke in a whispering voice, monotone and void of feeling, their naked coffee-colored branches clapping in the wind. From where I watched in the shadows, I could feel her angst. She was scared and confused. I believe she may have spotted me, and as I moved back slowly; she strained to see.

As she leaned forward, the limbs seemed to reach out and grab her, holding her in the swirling whirlwind of leaves, rain, and debris. Through the debris, she could see dark, sopping wet hair hanging over eyes that felt cold and dead. As she opened her mouth to scream, a voice cut through. We both heard it. It was calm, sweet, and safe.

“Simone? Simone? Wake up! You’re having that nightmare again. It’s alright. It’s just a bad dream. It’s alright.”

It was her sister, Clara. She’d woken Simone up again from the dreams. They’d become nightly visitors, the sort that were akin to unwanted guests.

Simone clung to Clara’s arms; the fear still in her round cocoa eyes as she sat up against the pillow. Clara pulled Simone’s head onto her shoulder as tears streamed down her face like the sheets of rain she’d left seconds before. It wasn’t a mere nightmare. To Simone, it had been so real, so vivid, so terrifying. And the eyes, the eyes haunted her.

He was going to screw this up, but I’d given this case to him as a favor. We all have our jobs to do, and this time mine is to oversee him. I can’t see how this is going to turn out as an act that balances karma, but I’m not sure it matters; given his conflict of interest. At least she's waking up again.

It happened every night, the same dream, continuing like a story. She would dream it, but it never felt like her own dream. I understood why she felt that way, but as of now I must simply observe and allow. This isn't my assignment.

***

Simone was in it, the one caught in the storm, but she never felt like it was really her.

Whose dream it was or what it meant, Simone had not been able to figure out. She was in the dream in every single scene and moment, but she still didn't know. She could never get far enough without waking up crying or screaming or both.

But every night it crept in when she was sound asleep to haunt her again, telling her something in a way too foreign for her to comprehend. There was always water, a storm, those eyes.

When she wasn't asleep, it was still there, lingering in the subconscious where she couldn't reach it and pull it out. Rather, it waited until the light left and night came in to crawl back in and greet her. It wasn't the way I would have done it.

Hours passed, the clock moving its hands from eleven to twelve to one as I watched Simone fight sleep madly, sitting up against the firm wooden headboard, trying not to drift off too soundly. But despite her attempts to avoid the deep sleep that brought the dream, it always managed to engulf her, afraid and alone, in its clutches. Once more, she fell asleep into the nightmare.

TWO

Simone

THE LEAVES SWIRLED, AND the wind blew harder. The black clouds moved in the heavy winds to gather above her head, and flashes of lightning and booming thunder stole the sky. She stood on an old wooden dock, with greying and rotting cracked panels. Large, gaping holes revealed the water beneath. At the end of the dock was a worn, yet beautiful, small, white boat.

Nothing this beautiful belonged here, and in this storm. In view of the boat, the structure she'd seen through the dark grey mist seemed to shift with the wind. Simone knew she wouldn't last.

While stuck in this dream, that small white boat with one sail torn slightly, having been battered by the winds, would have to be her shelter through the persistent storm. Simone struggled to walk towards it as the wind blew harder, causing the rain to obscure the fancily written words that were already too difficult to read without the rain.

> *I turned around in my hidden vantage point to find the source of the hard footsteps approaching. I wasn't supposed to be spying on him as he worked, but clearly I needed to keep an eye on him.*

Simone heard the heavy boots too. She sped up her pace towards the little boat that would be her safe haven. Then she was running...run ning for all the life she had in her as the heavy clunking boots made chase. For every one step the boots took, Simone had to take almost two. A clear disadvantage.

Her tears were hidden by the rain and her screams by the clapping and rolling thunder. She stumbled on a broken plank, blinded by her tears.

> *I looked on as she caught her toe and fell hard, crashing* face-first *to the wood.*

She left small blood droplets behind from the cut on her chin. She was now trapped and bleeding between the broken planks and the man on a mission. He was dressed in black from his top hat to his rubber galoshes.

"Are you Lana Fier?" the larger-than-life figure asked in a husky, dry voice that reminded Simone of cigars and bourbon in a lounge with swanky waitresses. She couldn't see him clearly as the rain and her tears masked his face. The shadow cast by the oversized brim of his hat, concealing his eyes. I recognized him.

"No, no. I am not Lana Fier! And what concern is it of yours?" She feigned belligerence, trying to shield how vulnerable she felt.

"You are Lana Fier!" he boomed.

His eyes grew wide and angry as he disregarded her question. He reached down, his fingers clasping the collar of her thin yellow rain jacket, and he yanked her up towards him. Her feet dangled inches above the ground and her face was so close to his she felt his hot breath against her nose.

His eyes were haunting, and the thick black brows pulled in to form lines above the bridge of his small, narrow nose. But those weren't the eyes that haunted her dreams. Similar, but not the same.

"No, I'm not. And even if I were, you still don't have the right to scare me like that and practically threaten my life. Who is Lana Fier?"

Simone tried to remind herself that she must be dreaming. It had to just be a dream. He couldn't hurt her in a dream, not really. Scare her? Yes. But she'd wake up. Soon, she hoped. Very soon.

"You should know; you conniving vixen. You seduced and killed my only brother, and you shall pay dearly for that deadly mistake," the words oozed out of his mouth like venom, and Simone could taste the poison on her tongue.

I was curious about how he would handle this. Simone's body quivered as shivers went up and down her spine. She'd denied being Lana Fier. Would he accept it? Could he accept it and move on? Or would he take this further?

Lana Fier. The name sounded familiar to Simone, but it didn't connect with anything she could readily recall in her moment of terror.

Out the corner of her eye, she saw me again. A figure lurking in the distance, beyond her clear view, watching as she was tortured by this crusader. I turned away, not wanting to

see the pleading eyes that sought out
my salvation.

"Yes, you shall pay Lana Fier. For all the life of you, for his, you shall pay!" This shattering statement woke her up, drops of sweat dripping from her brow, her pillow damp, yet a chill still running through her bones. Simone began to weep.

Lana

The confusion continued as Clara sat at the edge of the bed, near tears, watching as her sister slowly adjusted her eyes.

"What's wrong, Simone? Please tell me what's wrong. Please Simone, please."

Lana looked at her through a glaze of sleep-filled eyes. *Who was this strange woman and why was she sitting on her bed in the middle of the night?*

In the dark she favored one of her dorm-mates from down the hall, but why would Kathy be in her room at... she looked to the right to check the time. *Who moved the alarm clock? How was she supposed to wake up for her classes on time?*

"Simone, what's wrong?" Clara asked again.

"Kathy, my name is not Simone. It is Lana. Lana Fier! You should know that by now. We've been in the same dorm as next-door neighbors all semester. Now, what time is it? And who moved my fricking clock?"

"Simone! What is wrong with you? You want to have these nightmares and have me run in every hour to comfort you and then act like you don't know me? Your name is Simone, and it has been for the past eighteen years! Snap out of the dream."

"Pardon me. But I have not been eighteen for three years now! Good night, Kathy. I'm tired of the games. Go back to your room. I'm going back to sleep." Lana spoke into the dark room, annoyed that her alarm clock was missing and that Kathy felt the need to play games in the middle of the night. She fell back onto the bed and into a listless sleep.

Lana awoke in a frenzied state a few hours later. She threw the white duvet covers off her in a panic and snapped her head around to look check the time. The clock was still missing. She'd never make it to her...wait a minute. This was not her dorm room, and her roommate Taylor was not there.

> *She was in a state of confusion, and I wondered if Maxwell already knew. Lana was here, and he was now looking in the wrong place.*

Simone

Simone turned her head from one side to the other to avoid the sunlight that made her eyelids light up red from the inside. Brown waves fell over her face, helping to block some of the offending light.

She wasn't in the mood for school and the math test she'd have in Trigonometry. Despite studying, she was too tired to think straight.

She forced herself awake, slowly opening her eyes, rubbing the sleep away, and blinking as she tried to focus. Nothing looked familiar. "Where am I? How'd I get here?"

She looked around the cramped room that held a single twin bed with a simple wooden slatted headboard along one wall and another twin bed that matched the one she was in, against the other. Her eyes tried to make sense of what she was seeing before her heart began racing again.

The bed across from her had rumpled turquoise and white floral covers, and the pillow had fallen to the side. It now rested there, leaning against the mattress. She definitely wasn't in a prison. She had the fleeting thought that maybe she'd been kidnapped by someone really twisted but with a sense of style.

Whatever had happened, something was wrong. She promised herself she wasn't going to scream this time as she looked out the window. Below her and around her looked like the dormitories she'd often seen in movies. She hadn't woken up after all; she sighed with relief.

She moaned and wondered how deeply asleep she must be. She pinched the skin on the back of her forearm hard and winced in pain. It hurt. She wasn't asleep, and she wasn't where she was supposed to be.

Simone panicked as she wondered if she'd been kidnapped, drugged, and a number of other scenarios that could possibly explain how she wound up in that foreign place.

It was all unfamiliar. The buildings. The grassy area beneath the window that led to a sidewalk. A park in the distance was already beginning to fill with people carrying their life possessions in bags and baskets. The noises outside and the city skyline didn't make sense. She was on some kind of city college campus.

"No, that's ridiculous," I heard her whisper.

She thought again that maybe she was still dreaming. Simone heard her own nervous laugh escape her throat for thinking such a scary and stupid thing - her in Atlanta, at a city college campus and not in her Valdosta suburban home. It was laughable.

THREE

Lana, Age 18

HAND IN HAND, THEIR fingers were entwined. The two of them ambled without care through the lush expanse of trees and dense, sweet-smelling bushes. They picked blueberries along the way, the fruit bursting with tart, midnight-blue juice against their tongues.

Wildflowers now adorned Lana's thick, dark curls, which she had meticulously straightened and adorned with sun-kissed amber highlights just for Mickal. Mickal had picked each flower himself; his movements deliberate and reverent as he placed them over her ear.

One yellow for hope.

One white for innocence.

One red for love.

A warm flush rose to Lana's cheeks as he placed each one. When he came across the right colors, he whispered the meaning behind each bloom against the shell of her ear. Lana wished the moment could be paused, a snapshot of this perfect moment. She was sure her own parents didn't have memories like this.

As they continued their carefree walk, they stopped to touch the different trees and foliage. They would pause so that the crackling of their feet against the woods droppings on the ground wouldn't disturb the songs of the birds that made their home there. Lana thought about how loudly the birds chirped as they cried out to each other in warning. All the while, they talked of their love, their words weaving a soft cocoon around them.

The blue sky with swirled cirrus clouds painted like brushstrokes dotted the heavens above their heads, creating the perfect backdrop. The sun's rays splintered through the canopy, dancing in dappled patterns across their skin. Their rolled jeans were dusty at the hems, like their bare feet from the dirt path worn down, but now abandoned.

It was August, and school would be starting again for both of them, driving a wedge again between their love as they were forced to part.

Lana would be a senior in high school, and Mickal was starting his sophomore year of college. He had missed her terribly the previous year; their time reduced to stolen moments during short holiday breaks.

He'd even played with the idea of transferring back to a school closer to her so they could really be together. She, instead, had insisted that he finish up where he was. She didn't want to be the reason he sacrificed his future.

After their lazy walk through the woods, the trees pulled back and opened up to the beautiful park-like setting by the water. They'd reached their destination. It was a mostly forgotten man-made lake by the woods. The brush was overgrown, and Lana guessed someone only came out two or three times a year to tend to the area, but that didn't matter. To her, it was beautiful, peaceful, their special and secret place.

Flowers, flowers by the lake
Pick them. Let us know our fate
Hold me, never let me go
Flowers, flowers. Where'd they go?

Lana and Mickal sang their short, playful song with arms wrapped tight around each other, swaying as they looked into one another's eyes. Lana still struggled to believe she had actually landed Mickal, that a boy like him had truly fallen for a girl like her.

She'd never meant for it to go this far, but it had. They'd literally bumped into each other at a movie, and he'd accidentally spilled half of her popcorn on himself, on her, and on the floor.

She wanted to be mad, but then she looked up at him and his abashed smile. She saw that dimple an inch to the right of his lips, those soul-stirring, crystal blue eyes, and his all-around good looks, and the only thing she felt was mesmerized.

She wasn't supposed to be with someone like him, at least not according to her parents. He was everything she was told she shouldn't want, everything they feared. But standing there by the water, with the scent of wild honeysuckle thick in the air and Mickal's heart beating against her own, she didn't care.

FOUR

Lana, Age 18

MICKAL LOVED HER FIERCELY. He might have been the first person to ever really love her, to be willing to give it all for her. Do anything for her. She knew he would. She'd tested him and he'd passed. She'd managed to get him to fall in love with her, and over time she grew to love him back, in her way.

Robby Bill, RB for short, considered himself as being protective of his daughter and only child. He was a man built of grease, cold steel, and old grudges. RB had forbidden her to see Mickal the moment he realized how serious they were, and he'd clocked the way the boy walked with the easy, infuriating confidence of a Jonson. No daughter of his would date a boy from a family like that.

"The families have history," was all her father would say, his voice a low, gravelly rasp that sounded like metal grinding on pavement. That was the extent of his explanation, and it was that very secrecy that fueled Lana's pursuit of Mickal. It made him forbidden fruit, sweeter because of the venom her father tried to inject into the situation.

Her father wanted more for her, even if he couldn't be the one to give it to her. He was a man who had long ago traded his own dreams for a mechanic's uniform, and he refused to let his daughter take anything from the Jonson tree.

RB, Age 18

The air in the locker room smelled of socks, mud, and old sweat, but RB barely breathed. He laced his cleats, his hands trembling, not from nerves, but from a growing, disturbing realization.

Wesley Jonson sat three lockers down, surrounded by a ring of varsity players. He was laughing, tossing a football casually into the air, the golden boy in his natural habitat.

"Hey, RB," Wesley called out, his grin bright and easy, the kind that had charmed half the county. "You ready for the scouts? My old man says they're only looking for one thing today: flair."

RB didn't look up. "I'm ready to win, Wes."

"Win?" Wesley let out a sharp, dismissive laugh. "Winning is a given. You just need to make sure you're in the right place to watch the magic happen."

The coach pushed through the swinging doors, his clipboard a heavy slab of authority. He marched straight to Wesley, ignoring everyone else. "Jonson. You're the focal point today. We run the offense through you. Everyone else? You're just the stage dressing. Keep the lanes clear for him."

The coach didn't even glance at RB. He didn't have to.

The game was a blur of violence and frustration. Four quarters of running routes until RB's lungs burned, his hands ghosting over the air where the ball never landed. Every time he broke free, every time he found the soft spot in the secondary, the play went to Wesley.

With seconds left on the clock, RB found himself wide open in the end zone. He waved his arms, eyes locking onto the quarterback. Throw it, he thought. Just once.

The quarterback looked him dead in the eye, then pivoted. He lofted a lazy, looping pass toward the sideline where Wesley stood, covered by two defenders. Wesley jumped, snatching the ball with a predatory grace, and jogged into the end zone.

The crowd erupted. The scouts scribbled furiously.

When they hit the showers, the silence in the room was heavy. RB stood by the sink, scrubbing the mud from his face.

"Great game, right?" Wesley leaned against the row of lockers, already wearing his varsity jacket. "My dad said he saw me scouted for State by the end of the first half."

RB turned, water dripping from his chin. "You didn't see me open on that last play, Wes? I was standing alone in the end zone."

Wesley paused, his expression shifting from triumph to a cold, practiced indifference. He walked over and patted RB on the shoulder, a gesture that felt like a brand. "Maybe you were. But scouts don't pay to see the guy standing alone, RB. They pay to see the guy who makes the play."

He leaned in closer, his voice dropping. "It's not about how hard you work. It's about who you are. Maybe you should just learn to enjoy the show from the sidelines."

As Wesley turned to walk out, Shellie was there, waiting by the door. She looked at Wesley with a gaze that held no room for anyone else.

She glanced briefly at RB, but her eyes didn't linger—they had already moved on to the future.

FIVE

Kaela

I WATCHED THE CYCLE turn. It was a familiar and tired. Shellie left, thinking she'd found a golden ticket, only to be discarded when the shine wore off. It was almost poetic, seeing her get left exactly the way she had left RB.

Then came Angela.

She walked into town like a fever dream, all nervous energy and beauty that didn't belong in a place like this. She was lost, truly. We lower angels whispered about it. She was on an assignment that had gone wrong, and she was looking for a tether. She found one in Wesley Jonson.

He didn't just charm her. He consumed her. I saw them on the park bench two months later, her hand resting on a stomach that held the beginning of Max. She looked at Wesley like he was the only source of light in the world. He played the part perfectly. He was sweet, generous, and exactly the trap she needed to walk into.

But Angela was never meant to stay. One year later, she was simply gone, leaving a vacuum where a mother should have been and a squalling infant in a nursery that felt more like a warehouse.

Wesley looked at Max and didn't see a son. He saw an inconvenient error, a piece of evidence he couldn't quite sweep away. I watched him stand over that crib, his face hardening into the cold mask he wore when the public wasn't around.

He didn't have to raise the boy alone for long. He bought a wife, or as close to it as money and social standing can provide. When she delivered Mickal, his change was complete.

Mickal was the heir. He was the athlete, the charmer, the boy who carried his father's ego like a crown. And Max? Max became the ghost in the house. He was the one who scrubbed the mud off Mickal's boots and buried the secrets of his brother's late nights, always silent, always invisible.

Now, history is looping again.

Wesley paces his office, his jaw tight as he watches Mickal. He's terrified. Mickal has found Lana, a girl who represents everything Wesley didn't plan for. He wants to reach out and pull his son back to the path, to stop him from making the same reckless choices that marked his own youth. But he knows his son. He sees his own reflection in the boy's stubborn eyes. If he tries to break them apart, he will only weld them together.

He has no idea that the boy he ignores; the kid living in the background, is the only reason his perfect legacy hasn't already burned to the ground.

***

RB

RB *graduated and* got a diploma to fix cars. His dreams of college were cut short after they learned Lana was coming. They were young and didn't have much, but he prided himself on being one of the best mechanics in town. At least that's what his boss told him. Michael Jonson, Wesley's father, owned half of Main Street.

You couldn't get a job working in town unless you played by his rules, and RB had done that. He'd played by the Jonson's rules his whole life, and he would go sit under a shadowy cliff in the Arctic before his daughter got sucked up by them.

In RB's opinion, they were all pretentious, self-absorbed, arrogant, and entitled. All of their perceived entitlement still didn't entitle Wesley's son to think he could have his only child.

***

Lana

RB was such a hypocrite, Lana thought as she considered how romantic and perfect it all was. Mickal wasn't much different from her father, but RB wanted to act high and mighty and say Mickal wasn't good enough. They lived in the wrong part of town, the side of the tracks where those who worked for and serviced families like the Jonsons lived.

Lana wasn't stupid. She knew the truth. RB had never been good enough, given the scraps left behind by the Jonsons. Mickal was one of those Jonsons, and her mother, weak and often useless, never defended her choice to her father.

Her mother had married RB against her own parents' wishes after finding out she was having his baby. *Love child.* That's what Lana was, but there was never much love there. Her parents never had any more kids, leaving Lana alone to deal with the two of them.

SIX

Mickal, Age 19

MICKAL STEPPED BACK, CONTINUING to admire her as he took her hand. He loved her beyond reason and knew that he'd love her for the rest of their lives. He didn't care that she was still in high school. One year was nothing. It might be a hard sell, but he'd even wait, if he had to.

He took her soft hands in his, admiring the bright blue polish she'd put on for him. He slowly began moving down, placing one knee in the damp grass by the water.

"Lana Fier, my perfect flower; I have loved you since I met you a year ago today. I will always love you, Lana, and I hope that you will always love me. Will you make me the happiest man alive and be my wife?"

Mickal continued to kneel, the moisture soaking through his jeans as he waited, but he didn't seem to notice. All he could see was Lana. His Lana. Always his Lana.

He smiled up at her, looking into her almond-shaped brown eyes and waited for her answer. It could only be yes. She loved him as much as he loved her. He was certain of this.

Lana, Age 18

Falling in love with Mickal was her escape. In these moments with Mickal, she could pretend her sad excuse for a life wasn't real. Mickal had even snuck off secretly, skipping his weekend boat trip with some of his family and friends, to be with her.

Lana pulled up on Mickal's hands in a silent request for him to stand. Her words caught in her throat for a moment as she considered what he'd asked.

"Mickal. I do love you. We're too young. It wouldn't work out, you know that, right?"

"We're young but we love each other. Why not get married?"

"You're kidding, right?" she grinned. "You didn't think marriage was where we were going?"

"Don't you love me?"

"Of course, I love you," she said with compassion, leaning in to give him a kiss. His hand reached out stopping her.

"Then I don't understand the problem.

"I love you. I do and you know that, but we can't marry." She looked with compassion into his eyes, often laughing and cunning and filled with strength and passion. They reminded her of the sky on a clear day. Still she wasn't going to end up like her parents, trapped in a bad marriage.

His eyes shifted from hope to something else.

Mickal was fun and exciting, and dating him made her parents mad. That was enough of a thrill for now.

"We're young, baby. This is supposed to be free and fun."

"Free to do what? Be with other guys?"

"Really? That's what you think?"

He didn't understand, and that was part of the problem.

"Why else, Lana?"

She couldn't tell him that he was too much like her father. Tall, dark, and handsome, with a temper that sometimes left her with a residue of fear she could feel under her skin when he was passionate enough about something.

"I love you. I'm attracted to you, Mickal. There's no one else, but I have things I want to do in life."

She was wildly attracted to him, but there was this side of him that frightened and bewildered her. There was a mysterious essence to him that could engulf her in complete darkness if she wasn't careful.

"You wouldn't have to do anything you didn't want to do as my wife. Have a couple kids, secure the family tree, and be with me."

"I don't think we want the same things. I plan to go to college next year, so I have to secure my scholarship this year. No distractions, Mickal."

"I see. Me loving you is a distraction," he huffed. "Do you know how many other girls would love to be with me? For me to give them the chance to be a Jonson?"

"A lot. So why me?" She loved the idea of him. What being with him meant for her. She didn't love him in the way he loved her.

He said nothing. Studying the lines on his palm and the skin on the back of his hands, tanned by long summer days.

She couldn't bear the silence or to look at the sorrow in his eyes that now reflected grey. He turned his gaze to her. Avoiding his penetrating scrutiny she took out her pocket knife and grabbed a broken tree limb that lay near her foot. She'd whittle until he decided to speak to her. She knew he was angry. She could feel it all around him like fireworks shooting off towards her.

"Maybe we should head back," she said softly.

Lana took a step back from him and the hostile energy emanating from him. She'd said her piece, and he didn't like it. Instead of speaking, he stared, seething, his eyes trying to burn her soul, it felt. His eyes bored into her as she held the wood in one hand and the pocketknife in the other.

"You in a hurry all of a sudden? Thought you had the day."

"I just know you're upset, that's all."

"Of course I'm upset, Lana Fier. All this time and you've been playing me!" he growled. "You think I'm just some toy you can play with and then throw away?"

"It's not like that, Mickal," Lana said with hesitation.

Lana had broken him, belittled him. Made silly putty of his ego, and now she didn't even give him the dignity of her attention.

"You think you're too good for me? Can't even look at me while you lie?"

"Please calm down, Mickal."

"Calm down! After everything I've ever done for you, and it still wasn't enough!"

He lunged toward Lana, trying to grab the knife, but Lana's smaller, agile frame and speed wouldn't allow it; twisting around and escaping his reach.

"You stupid whore! You could've been one of us. Had everything. But no, you want your little pathetic life." He pushed her from behind instead, knocking her off balance and causing the knife to go careening from her hand, coming to rest a body's length away in the damp grass.

"Stop, Mickal! You're scaring me!"

Spotting the knife's landing point, Lana scrambled to pick up what was now a weapon.

"Good. You should be scared after what you did."

Mickal wasn't going to let her get it that easily. He lunged at her again, tumbling over her before she was able to grab it. The knife was at the tip of her fingers. Another half of an inch and it would be in her hand.

"Nobody does this to me. Not to a Jonson. Not in this town!"

He jerked her leg back towards him, spreading the gap to a hand's length. She covered the lost inches quickly after kicking him in the chin with the other leg. Lana had the knife in her hand, and Mickal was coming at her again.

Lana could only wonder for a split second what he was going to do. *Why was he acting this way? Was marriage that important to him?* No, she thought. She'd hurt his precious ego. His ego didn't trump her freedom. She would never be bound to a man like him.

Thoughts raced through Lana's head as he dove for her and knocked her back to the ground.

She'd seen it before. The struggle between a man and woman. His size was an obvious advantage over her. She thought about the scar her mother had on her left hip, left by one of the many episodes with her father that brought the police and ambulance coming. Her mother was clumsy and accident-prone. At least that was what the acceptable story was. She would not wind up like that.

"Stop! Stop, Mickal! What's wrong with you? You're acting...you're acting crazy! You keep coming and you'll regret it. I won't, but you will."

His eyes held a rage she'd never seen. He was about to reach for the knife, and instead she pulled it back and then drove it deep into his side. He continued to come toward her, ignoring the wound. His eyes still held the look of a wild animal.

"Mickal!" she cried out again, hoping to snap him out of this crazed state.

He reached his hand towards her and she plunged the knife into his side again, still not stopping him. As she held the knife out in front of him, warning him to stay back, he threw himself at her again. Unwilling to give up he tackled her to the ground, driving the small blade the full way into his heart.

Mickal pulled away from her in disbelief. He looked at her and her bloodied hands and then at the small knife. The blood poured over his button-down shirt as the small pocket knife still penetrated his chest.

He looked into her eyes, suddenly realizing what had happened. Anger and the sense that he'd been betrayed imprinted in his eyes before he fell back with shallow breaths, choking, and struggling for life.

Before his last breath escaped his lungs, he whispered with partly closed eyes, "You'll pay, Lana. You'll pay." These last words were like an echo by the lake.

He was gone.

Hold me, never let me go

Flowers, flowers. Where'd they go?

Seven

Lana, Age 18

Lana's body trembled as her mind returned from being driven by her instinctual need to survive.

"Oh, my God! Mickal! Mickal! What did I do? What did you do? Answer me, Mickal! It wasn't a lie. I do love you!"

She picked up his lifeless body and cradled it in her lap as she kneeled beside him.

"I...I just can't marry you. Don't you understand that, Mickal? You stupid brute. This is why I can't marry you. Why no one should. But I still love you."

She sobbed uncontrollably, caressing his cheeks still warm from the blood that had been heated by their battle. She pulled the lids over his blank eyes. Staring at Mickal's lifeless face through a sheet of tears, she knew he hadn't understood.

Lana sat in the damp grass, rocking Mickal's limp body. The shock of what had happened slowly began to wear off as she held the limp body on her lap. Reality began to set in that she'd killed her boyfriend, and she glanced around to see if there had been any witnesses to her crime.

Out here there was no one. There were only the birds and woodland creatures to bear witness. She would need to find a way to conceal his body.

She might never forgive herself or forget about what had taken place, and his blood would forever stain her hands; but she couldn't allow the rest of her life to be ruined because of his temper and stupidity. He'd made her do this.

He'd come after her and tried to get the knife. He had gotten too angry because he didn't understand.

Lana looked around her. There were the woods. She'd bury him deep in the woods! No, that would take too long. She would dig a large hole by the lakeside where the ground was softer and digging would go more quickly. That might work, but that would still take longer than she had.

If she weren't home before her parents got home from work, they would start worrying and asking questions. She would barely get through the door before the interrogation began. If RB had a bad day, it could get even worse for her.

She needed to get moving quickly. She looked at the small dock by the lake, in poor shape but usable. Hurriedly, Lana looked around her. There had to be something she could use.

Twenty-five yards from her, on the side of the lake, she spotted it. The oddly shaped, white-speckled rock about the size of a basketball would do what she needed. She ran over and struggled to lift it. As she carried it cumbersomely to where Mickal's body lay, all she could say to herself was, "But he was going to kill me."

She still wasn't convinced she'd done the right thing, but she'd done the only thing she knew to do to survive. She was angry at him for forcing her to do it. The guilt tried to clutch at her heart as she dropped the rock by his foot. She resisted guilt's grip as she did what she had to do.

She looked down at him now; the blood having left his face, and knew she would have to get over the guilt. Over him. How deceiving love could be.

She removed the pocketknife that still stuck out of his chest. She needed the shirt he was wearing. It felt like an eternity had gone by in the time it took for her to use his blood-stained shirt to tie the large rock against his body.

The rock sat inside his shirt, and she tied the ends of the shirt tightly around his calf. Double-knotting and triple-knotting the sleeves of what was once her favorite blue and grey plaid shirt, she secured everything in place.

Sweat poured down her nose and the side of her face. Her hair, which had been blown straight, now had ringlets around the edges. She lifted Mickal's heavy body and dragged it with the stone to the dock.

He still had the build from his high school football days, and those pounds now strained against her arms and legs. She could hear the banging and dragging of the heavy rock as she struggled slowly on the wooden planks.

Her body ached under the weight, but she couldn't stop. There was no other out. She caught her breath and wiped her eyes before picking up what remained of Mickal. At the edge of the dock that overlooked the murky waters covered in a thin layer of algae, she stopped and kneeled down beside him. He looked like he was simply asleep.

His dark hair crowned his head, and his thick brows no longer bore any memory of the anger that had caused this. She hoped that wherever he was now he would forgive her, or even better, forget her.

She kissed his pasty forehead softly, straightened her back, and with a strong push she rolled him in. The splash seemed to startle the birds again, and their chirping and singing were a deafening cry bearing witness to her crime.

Lana rose to her feet, the shaky dock beneath her, and with a new burst of energy from the adrenaline still pumping through her body, she sprinted back through the woods. The basket of blueberries beat against her damp and bloodied leg.

She ran from their secret place and the murderous crime she'd committed. The plunging of the knife continued to replay in her mind. She tripped and stumbled over the vines and stumps she'd so gracefully avoided on her way in, but nothing would slow her. She had to get away. His words and their song played over and over in her head as she ran.

"You'll pay, Lana. You'll pay." These last words were like an echo by the lake.

Hold me, never let me go

Flowers, flowers. Where'd they go?

Lana ran. What she didn't know was that the karmic cycle had already begun, the force winding its way through her body as she moved from their secret place. She'd been running ever since. But at some point, every race must end.

EIGHT

Simone

SIMONE LOOKED OUT THE fourth-story window of the sparsely decorated room again and became frantic. She needed to figure this out, but her mind was stuck. She still didn't know where she was or how she'd gotten here.

New questions sprang into her head as she considered the first questions. "Where's my mom? My dad? My sister?" The questions continued to pile up as she desperately tried to make sense of the senseless situation. The dorm room was empty.

Across from her was another bed. Along the wall above it were pictures and drawings stuck neatly to the wall. It was another girl. Simone recalled what she thought was a dream and realized it had happened. After snapping at the first girl, the girl in the picture had come over to her, and she'd done the same to her. *Great.*

There was no time to worry about who she'd managed to piss off in the middle of the night. She was thankful that neither of them was there while she tried to get her head on straight.

There were much more pressing questions. "Am I dead? Or in a coma and stuck in a bad dream? Or did someone put a spell on me? Or was I drugged? There has to be a reasonable explanation for me being in this foreign place and in this foreign body. Crap! What if I switched with someone?"

That girl clearly thought she was someone named Lana. She wondered if it were possible that Lana might be at her house and in her body.

The anxiety started to kick in as Simone considered some strange person walking around in her body at that moment. Someone else might be in her body, in her bed, in her bedroom, in her house - in her life. She needed to think straight, and a nice warm shower would hopefully do the trick.

Simone rummaged in the drawers for clothes to wear. What did college kids wear anyway? She decided to play it safe and grabbed a pair of black leggings and a sweatshirt. She threw them on the bed to put on after her shower.

After searching unsuccessfully around the bed, she found a big, plush, yellow towel hanging in the closet. Inside the organized closet were shoes she didn't think she could even walk in stacked nearly to the ceiling. "Crap. I know there are some tennis shoes in here. I'll find them after I can think clearly enough to look."

Lana

Lana let out a piercing scream that made Rebecca Locke come storming into her room with her hair standing on end and sleep in her eyes.

"What? What, Simone? What's wrong?" Simone's mom asked anxiously.

"Nothing. Sorry. I thought I saw a rat or something," she lied. Things were getting stranger and stranger.

"Honey, are you okay? You sure you're not getting sick? Maybe you should stay home today."

She felt Lana's head for a fever, but her temperature seemed normal. Lana, instead, had a confused, unfocused, and lost look in her eyes, and her head felt like it was spinning.

"Yeah, maybe I should stay home."

She lay back down on the snow-flake pillow and let the sunlight filter through the window and onto her face. Her eyes hadn't even been able to adjust to see the woman who'd come in to check on her. She spoke to her like she might be the mother of whoever's body she was in.

Lana flopped over onto her stomach and closed her eyes to clear her head. She waited for the nice woman to leave the room, and then turned back over and eased herself off the bed.

She glanced down at her hands and noticed the pink polish covering the nails. Ugh, *so boring, and they aren't even freshly painted.* She needed to stand up and see in the mirror above the dresser in the room. She tried to steel herself.

Peeking into the mirror and catching a glimpse of the person staring back at her, she had to catch her breath and cover her new mouth with her new hands before another scream escaped. She stumbled back onto the bed. She strained to drag herself off the bed again as the shock took hold of her legs.

She moved slowly back and forth in front of the full-size bed, trying to make sense of what she'd woken up to. There was the pretty pink and white bedroom. There was the nice woman and then there was the unfamiliar body that had her trapped. She needed to get control of herself.

"I've got to do something. No. This is just a dream, a weird dream - a very lucid dream. I just need to wake up," Lana said to herself as she slapped her cheek hard.

The stinging sensation that filled her face with the certainty that this was no dream. As her eyes focused and began to take in the rest of the room. Tennis shoes and socks were on the floor behind the door. Clothes were strewn over a chair. Photos of a happy teenage girl who looked like the girl she saw in the reflection dotted the wall.

A girl who had some strong similarities to her, but more from what she looked like in high school, if she squinted and turned to the side. No freckles. What the heck was going on? She was losing her mind. That was the only explanation.

Simone

Simone opened the dorm door a sliver and poked her head through the crack. The hall was nearly empty except for a girl with a robe and bathroom basket walking into a door. Simone hoped that was the bathroom and not her bedroom. From where she stood, she couldn't tell.

She closed the door, looking around for something like what she had, a basket with bathroom stuff she'd need to shower. Not seeing anything in the room, she swung the closet door back open and then found it on a small shelf to the side of the shoes. Okay. She would have to go out there and find the bathroom. Whether she wanted to or not. She needed to use the bathroom.

Simone walked past half a dozen doors before finding the one for the bathroom and showers. She took a deep breath and pushed it in, hoping she wouldn't run into anyone.

"Hey, Lana. Late night, huh? How are you feeling now? You were pretty out of it," a pretty girl with olive skin and a rush of long dark curls said as she walked past her towards the door.

That was the first one Simone had seen last night.

"Uh huh. I'm okay." It was all she could muster up. She realized it didn't even classify as a thought as it came out with her lips barely parted.

Simone rushed into the stall to empty her bladder and escape before coming out again to shower. She waited in the stall, safe behind the doors, as she heard voices come and go, talking about school, midterms, boyfriends, and the party that happened last night.

She stood there, still, her head against the side of the stall, and listened, waiting for them all to leave. When the talking ended, she looked under the stall and then made a beeline dash for the shower. The sound of her exhale at reaching this next safe spot could've been heard in the hall.

Simone had to get home. She couldn't survive here. She wanted her life and her body. It was more than a want. She needed her life and her body. The thought of classes, teachers, tests, and a campus of strangers made her nauseous. She had to figure out where she was and then figure out her way back home, one way or another.

The water from the shower ran over Simone's back and splashed her hair before she threw a cap over the curls. Then the water hit the plastic and ran down her neck. She leaned her head forward, letting it hit her shoulders, and then turned her head up and let it run over her face.

Simone's hands felt for the wall behind her, and she lifted the shower head as she leaned back and let it rain down on her. No answers had come yet, but they had to be there. There was an explanation for all of this, but Simone hadn't thought of it yet.

I wanted to give her a clue, a tip to help her get her questions answered. It looked like the shower had given Simone a boost and she was feeling a little better. I could see a little more life beneath her brown skin, but she was still clearly not in her right mind

> *since the mirror by the sinks kept showing her someone else's face, startling her yet again.*

Simone grabbed the basket with the shower gel and face wash and opened the bathroom door a crack. As she looked through, strands of wet hair hung in front of her where they'd escaped the cap she'd hastily put on. She dashed to the room that she'd woken up in, flung the door open, and ran inside, slamming it shut before collapsing in a heaping wet mess on the threadbare carpet-covered floor.

NINE

Simone

"CALM DOWN, SIMONE. YOU'LL make it home fine," she said aloud, trying to ease her own fears and doing a terrible job.

The tears started trying to leak from her eyes again, but this time she forced herself to put on a stern face while she searched for the courage that was hidden somewhere inside. She pulled herself off the floor, holding onto the bed she'd found herself in and sat on its edge.

> *I wanted to come in and help her. Sit next to her for a moment so she could feel that it would be alright, but this wasn't my direct assignment. The situation hadn't reached a point critical enough for me to take* control, *and it wasn't bad enough that a request for help would be answered. I guess it was something those above me thought she could still handle on her own. She's* so young, *though.*

The dresser with Lana's clothes stood in front of a frameless oval mirror mounted to the wall. As she garnered the courage to really look at the face in the mirror, she began to study it. Tiny freckles dotted her brown nose, spilling over to her cheeks slightly. The lips were a little thinner than hers, and the teeth probably had never seen braces.

She felt like she was looking at an older version of herself or an older sister, if she had one. It made no sense. Had she somehow time-traveled? Skipping her senior year and even some of college?

She looked down at the rest of herself, staying covered in the yellow towel.

She was embarrassed. The toes were painted the same fuchsia color as the nails on her hands. They both looked like they had benefited from regular pedicures and manicures. She shook her head.

What did she care about that for? Not only was she in a foreign place, but now she didn't even have her own body. How would anyone believe she was actually the daughter of Jacob and Rebecca Locke?

Simone was devastated as the sensation of defeat began to crawl through the body holding her mind. I shook my head as I heard Simone think she might as well be dead. Then she thought that maybe she was dead, and *this was some sick, twisted version of hell.*

"Screw you!" she yelled at the girl looking back at her in the mirror. Then she thought about the dreams.

> *Reminding her of the dreams was the only hint that I could send as a simple subliminal message – my spirit to hers.*

That tall man with the black hat; maybe this had something to do with him, Simone thought.. He'd been convinced that she was someone named Lana Fier. It was possible he'd made her into someone she wasn't. It was possible he'd taken Simone's identity and abandoned her in some alternate reality as a college student.

Her identity. The one thing that separated her from the more than seven billion other people on Earth. Simone slipped to the floor and burst into tears. It was too much, too much for her barely legal brain to handle.

She wanted her mother right at that moment. She'd never dreamed of the day that she'd admit to wanting her mom to be there or anywhere with her willingly.

> *From here I saw it. She was vulnerable and* afraid, *and that upset her. And with all of* that, *she was caught in some sick trap with no identifiable escape. All I could do now was watch and wait.*

Simone began to feel anger rising in her as she thought of the tall man in the top hat who'd most likely done this to her. The strange man who'd haunted her dreams night after night and been in her subconscious day after day. She would find him, and he'd undo whatever curse he'd done. But before she could find him, she needed to know where she was and had to get out of here.

Then she could hunt him down and make him realize he was messing with a real person – the wrong person. She hadn't done anything to him or anyone else. She would do all that as soon as she got out of here. But first she had to find out where here was.

The window of the dorm room faced a park. If she were where she thought she was, she was a long way from home. She sat back down on the unmade bed with the striped black and grey comforter. Before she could stop herself, the tears had come again. This time uncontrollably. She slid off the bed to the floor and rested her head against the side of the bed as she sat there in that big yellow towel.

Simone looked up to see Taylor come in. She stopped when she saw Simone slumped on the floor, tears running down her cheeks. She put her hands on her hips and said nothing as she kicked the door closed with her heel.

Through the sobs that were finally starting to end, Simone managed to get out, "Do you have a map?" She couldn't look Taylor in the eyes after her earlier behavior, but hoped Taylor wouldn't hold it against her.

"Yeah. What do you need it for? Goin' somewhere? Ready to say what your problem is?"

Taylor answered with very little forgiveness in her voice. She wasn't going to make this easy.

"I know. I'm sorry. I guess I'm a little tired."

"Well, next time you want to snap on someone trying to help you calm down from one of your crazy dreams in the middle of the night, I'll stay right over here, in my bed. You can snap on Kathy. I don't need it, really. Had me up all night the past three nights with your moaning and huffing and crying," she said, looking out of the corner of her eye as she picked up her tablet and opened the maps application.

She was taking forever. It was as if she were purposefully moving at the most leisurely speed possible to cause Simone more agony. Simone wished she would hurry up. The feeling of being in a time warp made her head spin. She felt like she was standing in the top of an hourglass, and the sands were running low, about to suck her through to the bottom. Finally, Taylor pulled it up and handed it to her.

"Here. Where are you going anyway?" she asked again.

Taylor watched Simone closely as Simone darted her own eyes to avoid Taylor's inquisitive stare. Simone couldn't help but think, 'If only she'd get off my case and leave me alone.'

> *Even I would have a hard time explaining to Taylor what was happening to Simone. Simone didn't even know what was going on for* sure, *and there were no words she could find yet to use.*

"Thank you," Simone said, entering her home address painfully slowly as she tried to work with the unfamiliar fingers on the unfamiliar hands.

The location marker showed the campus, and then the map moved to her home address. She was where she thought she was - downtown Atlanta. The zooming went in as the miles stretched.

When the map finished loading and calculating the directions, it was a 250-mile drive back home, to the other side of Valdosta. She'd never make it back, not by herself. Simone had to find Lana's identification and money, and her phone. If she could find those things, she could catch the bus back.

"Can you call me? I can't find my phone." Simone now felt sheepish and silly with her requests to Taylor.

Taylor sighed and then picked up her phone to call Lana. Simone sat quietly, waiting for it to ring. After a few seconds, she picked up the faint sound of buzzing and vibrating. Simone crawled along the floor to the closet, following the sound, and then opened the door. The light from the phone lit up the clothes above as it lay on the floor near the back. It must have fallen out of Lana's pants before they switched.

"Thanks so much," she said to Taylor with a slight glance up and what might have been mistaken for a little smile.

Simone turned the phone on and was met with a lock screen. "Crap. What's the fricking password?!" she muttered louder than she thought.

I knew it wasn't fair, she was stuck.
But I couldn't help but chuckle a little.
I have to find my moments of humor
in all this madness, otherwise I'll go
mad.

"You forgot your password?" Taylor said, laughing right along with me, though she couldn't see me as she shook her head at the same time. "You need help, girl. I'm sorry."

"Wait. Where are you going?" Simone asked frantically.

"I'm gonna be late for my next class. So are you, by the way. If you can't remember it, you can always try to do a system reboot. You'll lose everything though, but that's the breaks."

Taylor grabbed a big chemistry textbook off her desk and threw it in her backpack before walking out the door.

TEN

Simone

SIMONE LOOKED BACK OUT through the window panes. A moment later she saw Taylor head out the downstairs door and begin her trek across the street. She threw on the jeans and the sweatshirt she'd left on the bed and then walked back over to the neatly organized closet where she found a pair of tennis shoes tucked in the back corner of the closet.

Simone had to find the wallet, purse, or whatever Lana put her things in, but had no idea where Lana would put them. After several hours in her body, she knew nothing about this girl, and yet she was her - for right now, at least.

She continued her hunt for Lana's license and wallet. All the while the thought going through her head was that this girl was probably screwing up her life back home. Simone hoped Lana didn't go to school today.

Simone could only imagine how she was making out as a high school student if she had. Or if Simone's mom, dad, and sister would realize something was off. The tall man's face flashed in her head again. "Yes, I'm coming to find you too," Simone muttered.

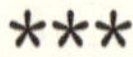

Maxwell

"She's trying to escape, but I will have justice. For you, Mickal. She will not get away with this. And I get to act on the highest authority," the tall man said through clenched teeth as he sat drinking from a brown bottle, looking at a picture of his brother Mickal on his phone.

He sat in the parking lot outside the dorm where Lana stayed. This was the one thing he needed to do before moving on, and it had already taken three years of his life . He took a deep breath and tried to regain his composure. I hoped he understood what was at stake.

The man opened the door to his gray late-model sports sedan and stood up slowly, letting his long legs and body stretch out to its full length. He was an ominous figure with crystal-clear blue eyes like the sky reflecting on ice.

He was not a bad-looking man, but for three years he'd been living on the idea of avenging his brother's untimely death, and it had taken a toll on his otherwise handsome appearance.

> *Now there was a darkness that seemed to take up residence in him* that, *even to me, at times felt threatening. For years I'd patiently waited for him to complete this* task, *and*

> now, *with three years of planning his* revenge, *it was finally in* action, *and something had gone wrong, putting an innocent at risk. He has no idea how pissed I am at him.*
>
> *He thought he'd found Lana Fier, but the girl last night had denied it. Now he wasn't sure. If Lana Fier* was still *out there, he would find her. Lana was supposed to have awakened in a different timeline, not a different* body, *but he needed to be the one to find her to know what exactly happened. I knew he wouldn't stop until this was done. He would come for Lana in this life or another.*

The tall man had decided that Lana was not going to get away with it any longer. But, if he had mistakenly switched her in this timeline with someone else, he needed to find her fast and fix it, otherwise, the mistake would be permanent.

He ran his long fingers over his black hair, angry at himself for possibly making such a serious error that could now delay justice even more. An error that, if he didn't correct, would have irreversible repercussions for everyone. He couldn't let that happen. He couldn't let his brother's murder go unanswered. He needed to know, for sure.

Simone

Simone turned to look back out the window once more to see if Taylor had really left. She didn't want to be alone. Taylor had now made it all the way across the park that sat a block away from the dorm, and was walking down the sidewalk.

As Simone looked back across the city, she'd only visited a couple of times in her life, she'd never seen it from this view. So much had changed since she was here for a hockey game before the city lost the team.

Her eyes passed the neighboring parking lot as a tall man got into a grey car and vanished down the street. There was something familiar about him, hauntingly familiar. Simone tried to remember where she'd seen him before.

The memory was there, she knew it, below the surface. All she saw was black - a man in all black. There was a black wool fedora hat on his head. It wasn't the top hat, but this was real life.

Eleven

Simone

"No!" THE YELL ESCAPED her lips before she could catch it.

Simone hoped the other nosy neighbor from last night didn't come back in to check on her. She needed some time alone, to think.

"It can't be! He was only a dream. A person in a dream!"

Simone shook her head as the sight of the man from her dream suddenly made it all too real. She thought it might be possible but seeing him put it in her face and she knew she had to get out. Fast.

"Lana! Lana! Girl, I know something is wrong with you now. Cuz you aren't acting right. You have got to calm down and talk to me - and don't tell me you suddenly need to go to the bathroom cuz you just went!" Taylor said.

Simone wondered how long she must've sat there in shock. When Taylor had shaken her shoulder, she'd been rocking herself, her arms wrapped around her knees, in the fetal position. Taylor had managed to get to her class and come back and she was still in the same place, by the window. Lost and scared. She'd done nothing to get herself out of this mess.

"I can't."

"You can and you are," Taylor said looking strong and confident.

Those were two things Simone could use at that moment. But Simone knew Taylor would never believe it. Switched identities? No one would ever believe her. If Simone told her, she might be worried enough to report her, and Simone could wind up taken in for some psyche profile and then who knows what would happen?

"I can't..." Simone said holding her hand up to stop Taylor from insisting any further. "I don't think you or anyone else would ever dream of understanding what happened to me or Lana."

"What do you mean 'me or Lana'? You are Lana."

"See, you could never understand. You're already doubting me," Simone said feeling justified for not trusting her.

"Look, Lana, no matter how big the problem is, I'll help you out," Taylor said trying to soften her tone.

"You promise? Can you promise that you'll never breathe a word of this to anyone else? I mean no one. No friends or family or anyone. Do you promise to help me even if it seems crazy?" Simone asked moving closer to her.

"Now you're scaring me," Taylor said, her stance tightening.

"Just promise me, you won't tell anyone."

"Fine. Yes - to all of that. Now what is the problem?" Taylor looked and sounded so serious now. She was all business.

"I don't even know where to start. It's all so confusing," Simone uttered desperately.

"Well, I always think it's easiest to start at the beginning," Taylor smiled.

"I'll start from the dreams, or should I say nightmares."

"Wait. Does this have to do with some dreams about a tall guy and lots of storms? If it does, I'm outta here." Taylor went to stand.

"You promised you'd help; whatever it was," Simone said reminding her of what she'd said a minute before.

"Okay. Fine. I'll listen, but I can no longer promise I'll understand."

"Fair enough. I'll start from last night and work on up to today. Last night I had a dream, not unlike many dreams before, that a tall man dressed in black was out to get me. He said that I was Lana Fier, and that I had killed his brother. But it was only a dream. I'd been in this kind of dream before and I figured it would end with me waking up, like usual. I hadn't killed anyone."

"Interesting. I know you've been having some strange dreams. Keeping me up with you," Taylor nodded at Simone.

"Well, I wasn't Lana Fier before last night. But today was different. I did wake up but I didn't wake up as me. Apparently, I woke up as the girl he thought I was. How does that happen? I know that I didn't kill anyone and I'm not going to pay for someone else's crime. Or for something he thinks happened when it didn't."

"That is strange. Unbelievably strange. Not that I don't believe you," Taylor added quickly, "but you have to admit it is a bit unbelievable. And that there are other explanations."

"I know it is and now I'm stuck in the body of this person he is hunting for killing his brother!"

"So, Lana, I mean, whatever. You were out late last night and partying. It's possible you're having some strange side effects. Maybe you should go to the health clinic."

"I'm not sick."

"But before we jump to body snatchers, maybe we cover the more practical options?"

"I don't have time to rule out everything I already know isn't the problem. I'm not Lana Fier. My name is Simone."

"Simone? Like Simone Midler?"

Simone huffed. "Yes. Now, I need to get back to me. Who know what this Lana is doing in my body, especially if she did what this guy is after her for."

"I'm not buying this story so fast but are you accusing Lana of actually being a murderer? If you are accusing her, and you're not Lana, then where is she and who the hell are you?"

"Yes, we did. I'm not the one accusing anyone of anything and Lana is probably at my home as me, Simone Locke. I'm eighteen years old and I live 250 miles south of from here, outside of Valdosta." Simone sent up a quick prayer hoping Taylor would believe her.

> *I looked around to see if anything would happen and if it was okay for me to jump in now. Nothing. The situ-*

ation still didn't require my intervention.

"By the way, I'm Taylor, since you may not be in the right mind to remember things like that. And yes, this is crazy. Absolutely crazy and I gotta say, I don't know that I'm buying it. It doesn't make sense."

"See. That's what I thought. If you don't believe me fine. Just play along as if Lana was in some trouble. Because if I am, so is she.

"I'll go along, for now. But, if you're lying don't ever come to me for help or anything else, ever again. I won't ever speak to you again. Got it?" she said sitting down next to Simone on Lana's bed.

"I got it. Because I'm not lying. This is unbelievable. This is crazy, I know. But it's real."

"What exactly did this guy say about Lana?" Taylor asked Simone still testing her story. She put a hand up to her forehead to feel for a fever, but she felt normal.

"He said she killed his brother! I don't have his name or the tall guy's name either. I saw him though, this morning. He was walking to a car in that parking lot across the street. It looked like he was leaving from this direction. Do you think maybe he was here? In this building?"

"There's no way Lana would or could kill anybody. I don't care if it was Adolf Hitler. She wouldn't kill him. She's too nice." Taylor was still in disbelief that Lana would have done the thing she was accused of. There had to be another explanation or some major misunderstanding.

Simone wasn't sure how she was supposed to find Lana now if Taylor didn't even believe it was possible Lana could commit such a serious crime. Of course, why would she think the girl she shared a room with could be capable of murder? Simone realized how stupid and utterly fantastical it all sounded.

"Look, I don't know Lana, or how she acts or thinks or anything else about her. All I know is that there was a dream, and a man told me I was Lana Fier and that Lana Fier had killed his brother and would pay for it. I woke up this morning in this place. Apparently in downtown Atlanta on a college campus and in her body!

So you have to help me find her since you know her. You may not like this very much but look at me. Put yourself in my shoes. Her shoes. I'm not even myself anymore," Simone pleaded.

Simone pushed back the tears.

"I can't do this without you, Taylor."

She was all alone in this big, strange city and had nothing to get her home, not even herself.

"Alright. You've gotta pull yourself together, girl. I'll try to help you, but if this gets too freaky, I'm gone. You got that?" Taylor pointed a long dark finger with lime-green nails at Simone.

"Thank you! Thank you! Thank you! All we have to do is have him turn us back to ourselves. The one problem is that, first we've gotta find him. He has to be pretty close, though. He didn't leave the parking lot more than ten or fifteen minutes ago," Simone said optimistically.

"Tell me how he looks, and I'll see if I can make a sketch. Be as descriptive as you can. Any details, all details matter."

"Well, he's really tall, maybe six and a half feet, and he wears a top hat. Well, today he had on a black wool Fedora hat," Simone began.

Taylor wrote down what Simone was saying on a piece of paper in her chemistry notebook before continuing.

"He wore black dress boots, but in the dream he wears galoshes and his hair is black. Thick and wavy. It's kind of perfect hair. His eyes...his eyes were so blue and clear, but they had a hint of evil in them. They were cold like ice and normal, not big, not small, but in the shadows of those thick brows. When he walked he took long strides and walked hard. I guess that doesn't help with drawing a face sketch."

"It's okay. Keep going," Taylor said, trying to reassure Simone.

I thought about his eyes. They could be considered a little evil looking, but they were still a very cool shade of blue. I don't think he knew how he came off, and right now I'm pretty sure he doesn't care.

"What's his face shaped like? Is it fat, thin, square, round?" Taylor asked, her pen sitting on the paper, ready.

"He has a square jawline, but his head isn't big. He was an average build. Oh yeah, he's kind of pale. No beard or mustache,, though. His nose is thin. He's strong. His face even looks strong - hmmm, strange. That's all I can remember," Simone said, feeling as if she'd failed some sort of oral exam.

"I should be able to do something with that. But you can always tell me where it's messed up. You know what you should do while I get started? Call home. Lana should be there, right? You two could go ahead and solve this together, and it would probably go a lot faster."

Simone didn't know why she hadn't thought of that before. It was plain she wasn't thinking clearly.

"You can use my phone since, ummm, you can't get into yours."

Simone looked at the phone sitting on the bed. She hadn't even tried doing the system reboot, probably because she'd been somewhere in a trance while Taylor was gone. Simone took Taylor's phone and started pressing the numbers for home.

She paused after entering the area code. What was she even going to say? 'Hi. I'm Simone

Locke and you're me?' No. 'Hello, I'm Simone Locke and right now we are in each other's bodies.' Yeah. That was pretty good and said it all.

Simone finished pressing the last digits and let the call go through. Eternity seemed to hang in the balance as the phone rang.

TWELVE

Lana

LANA STARED AT THE phone as it buzzed and rang in her hand. It was Taylor. She'd somehow found her. It must mean that whoever's body she was in was calling from Taylor's phone. Lana questioned if she should even answer it. She kept looking at the phone, feeling it vibrate in her palm as she paced around her new surroundings.

Finally, after what seemed like a minute the music ringtone stopped. Simone had crappy taste in music but she'd fix that. She put the phone down and it immediately began ringing again. After about thirty seconds she decided to answer.

"Hello?" Lana said, speaking softly but still with a slight edge to her voice. She couldn't be sure that Simone's mother wasn't outside the door.

"Hello. Is this Lana? This is Simone."

The line went silent. , and Simone wondered if it was because she had a bad connection.

The phone rang a third time and Lana considered letting it go to voicemail but feared the message the girl Simone might leave behind and she didn't know the passwords.

"What?" she said in a huff.

"I think we had a bad connection," Simone said quickly.

"No, I just didn't want to talk," Lana replied, without emotion.

"Please don't hang up. This is Simone Locke."

I perked up anxiously. She'd answered Simone's call this time and hopefully

> *wouldn't hang up on her again. I was already furious that Lana had hung up on her the first time. From where I watched, I could only try to control my overall irritation at the entire fiasco.*

"This is Simone, you say? How can that be when I'm right here?"

Simone looked at the phone in disbelief.

> *I looked at Lana. She wasn't upset enough about this switch and what it meant. I could see she was a little too comfortable with the situation.*

"Why would I lie to you? I have no reason. I just want my body back, and I'm sure you want the same thing. Right?" Simone said quickly.

"Well...actually...not really. I'm thinking you've got a pretty good life going for you here, from what I see. Your mom came in to check on me early this morning when I woke up, and so did your sister. Both seem really nice and caring. My parents would've let me scream or come in to tell me to shut up because I was keeping them up. No, I'm not in a rush to get back in that body," Lana spoke arrogantly into Simone's phone as she ran her hands over the pretty comforter. "This could be my do-over."

Simone and Taylor stared at the phone being held by this stranger's hands, both in disbelief.

Lana continued speaking as Simone could hear her picking up and putting down things in her room.

"This gives me a chance, a second chance at a good life. One without all the drama and the past holding me down. Any mistakes I might have made will be erased, and I would never have to worry about it. You know?"

"No mistakes are erased. They still exist. What are you talking about? A second chance? This is your life, and that is mine!" Simone shouted, surprised by what she was hearing.

"I didn't live such a charmed life. You...well you have a nice home, a nice family, and really nice things. I'm betting you even have nice friends. But enough of that. The life I have...no, the life I had, is now all yours. The drunk fights, the calls to the police, the yelling and the screaming. Enjoy being away at school, cuz home's a mess. It can get to be a bit much. Lucky for you, I got a partial escape with my full ride, and I've got a good part-time job. You have all that."

"No! I don't want your life. I want mine. You can't steal someone's life and get away with it!"

"I didn't steal your life. It was given to me. Cheer up now. You get to be done with college soon and live out your life. Unfortunately, you also get to deal with obnoxious parents, but only as you want and without all the built-up emotional baggage. Not a bad trade. But yeah, I don't want it back," Lana said smugly.

Simone listened, bewildered and in a state of confusion as to how the call could take a turn like this.

"No!!! You can't do that! It's not fair! I don't want your life and I'm not gonna pay for mistakes you made. Taylor must not know you very well. She said you were nice and would never kill anyone. Well, you're about to kill me now. It'll be for no reason, and it'll be your fault if I die. Do you want that kind of guilt?" Simone reeled, finding her voice but still sounding frantic.

Taylor watched as Simone paced back and forth, and the realization of what was happening sank in.

"Doesn't matter. I can live with it. I've done it before, and whatever guilt I might feel, if any, will pass. It'll fade over time, trust me. I once almost felt guilty over something that happened, but then I realized it wasn't really my fault. I let it go, then. Like this isn't my fault. I didn't do this to us. As for Taylor, I liked her, so I treated her nice. But I don't know you, so I can't like you. I like your life, though, so I plan to keep it." Lana sat on the plush beanbag chair and let it mold to her body.

Lana Fier had no intention of Simone getting her Barbie doll life back, not if she had anything to do with it.

"Bye, Lana. I really do need to go. Oh, and my middle name is Evilyn. That's E V I L Y N," she said, spelling it out with perfect enunciation. "Have a good life." The phone was silent again.

THIRTEEN

Simone

SIMONE AROSE SHAKILY FROM her spot on the floor while staring at her now reflection in the dark screen of the phone. The phone dropped from her hand to the bed. She sluggishly sat next to it on the bed and continued to stare at Lana Fier's face in the oval dresser mirror.

"Taylor?"

"Yes?" her tone told Simone she already knew.

“I don’t believe this,” Simone’s garbled words were barely audible.

“Neither do I,” Taylor shook her head in disbelief.

“She doesn’t want to switch back. She wants to be me. What am I supposed to do? I don’t want her life, especially now. She doesn’t even want her life.” Simone’s body crumpled onto the pillow as she stared at the white-speckled ceiling.

“Maybe your best bet is to go along with this. You know what else? If you find the tall man, chances are he’ll think you’re Lana and go after you. He’ll probably do something to your body though. I can’t believe Lana could do something like this. I’m shocked.”

“What if he kills me?”

“Then your brains will probably switch back or something like that. Your mind would be back in your body and her mind would be snatched out of your body. You know what I mean? Your body would be yours again, and her body would be hers again. I mean, I don’t know for sure, but you gotta find the man," Taylor said, sounding excited about the possibility.

"The key word there is probably. He could kill this body and me right along with it." Simone felt sadness dripping over her like the rain from her nightmares.

"But if you are right, then Lana would be dead. Obviously, she would have rather let me die. Why should I care about her anyway? I didn't ask to be in this, did I? I didn't kill anyone. I should turn her in to him and make him switch us back, and then she's all his."

"That's right, girl. You got your own life to live. You can't worry about her cuz she sure isn't worried about you!" Taylor got up and went to the notebook on her bed.

"It's not right. Either way, it's not right. I shouldn't be here, and she shouldn't be there, and no one else needs to die," Simone sighed, trying to find some place of reason in all this mess. "Did you get started on the sketch?"

"Yeah, it's still pretty rough though," Taylor said, shrugging her shoulders as if it were nothing. Simone looked at the amazing picture she'd put together. It was impressive. Simone hesitated to ask what Taylor's major was, but she could've been a professional artist.

Simone looked at the drawing in front of Taylor. "This is great. I think you are really close. It's actually really good. He looks a little too friendly, though, but it's him. I know! Let's go to the office in this building and ask if this man was here. We can ask why he was here and maybe get some more information, perhaps like a name."

Simone was excited to finally have something to go on. There was a picture she could show. She smiled a real smile for the first time in this new life.

"That's a good idea. Hopefully, Mr. Jenkins asked some questions if this man came in. He'd be hard to forget," Taylor said, smiling some and joining Simone in a momentary celebration.

The reflection looking back at Simone in the mirror had puffy eyes. Her curls hadn't been touched after snatching off the shower cap. Simone pulled it back into a mess of a bun and was ready to go. What she looked like didn't really matter much.

"Okay. I'm ready. Let's go." Simone was halfway out of the door before realizing Taylor needed to lead the way.

FOURTEEN

Lana

LANA WOULD NEVER HAVE to go back to her rotten life. By a random stroke of luck, she had been given a second chance. A new beginning. Someone else could deal with her problems now. She wouldn't have to deal with her parents, especially her dad. She would never have to deal with Maxwell again either.

He couldn't let it go. Three years had passed, and the only thing that now haunted her about that day was Maxwell. At least it was only through the dreams. They had only started in the past year, and for a moment she thought it had all caught up with her.

She wasn't surprised that something had finally happened with Maxwell. Mickal had always described him as overprotective. Even though Mickal was in college then, Maxwell always thought he had to come to his rescue if anything happened. But it had taken a turn for the better.

They were all out of her life now that she was out of her body. There was nothing Simone could do. The way Lana figured it, if Maxwell killed her old body, Simone's mind would die with it. The mind was in the body; no crossing back.

It felt so good to be given a second chance. Like a miracle. You don't give back miracles, and she didn't plan on giving this one back, and she wasn't going to waste it. Her mind was a few years wiser. She didn't have to make the same mistakes.

She still knew nothing about her new life outside of what she saw out in the open in the room. But she was eager to find out all she could so she could start living it.

She hadn't even met her new father yet. She had no idea what school she went to or what it would be like. Despite not knowing fully what to expect, she knew it had to be better than what she'd come from.

There had to be tons of information in here. Lana sat on the floor and reached under the bed. A pair of dress shoes came out. "Not bad. Not high enough, but okay."

She reached her hand under again and pulled out a blue notebook. There were only doodles in it. She looked around the room for other places that might hide clues to who she was.

A large black purse hung on the bedpost. She picked it up and popped the clasp, dumping the contents onto the floor in front of her. Out came a small red wallet followed by two tubes of lipstick, a compact, a small bottle of perfume, and a couple of pads.

She unsnapped the wallet and checked inside. Three dollars. There was nothing useful there. She left the items spilled out on the floor as she stood up to get the phone again.

She needed to get inside but without the password she couldn't. She considered the perfect princess bedroom she was in. It wasn't beyond reason that maybe Simone's mom knew the password. Simone seemed like the type who would give it to her mom in case.

Lana looked in the mirror at the cute eighteen-year-old and then she looked at the home screen picture of Simone with the girl Lana assumed was her sister. They looked like sisters, at least. She hoped the sister wouldn't be a problem and that the parents wouldn't be suspicious. She tried to mimic the smile and the eyes of that picture before walking out of the room in search of her new mom.

"Mom?" Lana yelled out into the hall. After stepping out of the bedroom, she didn't know where anything in the house was, including her new parents' bedroom. She walked slowly down the hall, listening for clues. "Mom?"

"Down here, honey. I'm cooking," Rebecca called back.

Lana followed the voice down a set of open stairs that led to a bright and cheery living room that opened up to the kitchen. A large, flat-screen television was mounted on the wall, playing the Home and Garden Network.

The bay windows were high, and the sunlight spilled into the room. As she descended the last step, she spotted the woman who'd come in earlier to make sure she was okay.

The woman who bore a strong resemblance to the girl's body she was in, her body, smiled at her. "I was going to call you in a minute and see if you felt up to having a late breakfast."

"I was coming to ask if you have my password. I can't remember it for some reason," Lana said trying to smile.

"Oh? Again?" the woman laughed sweetly. "I guess it was a good idea for you to send it to me, just in case, right? Hold on. Let me get my phone."

Lana could only think how lucky she was that Simone trusted this woman that much. Lana had never experienced trust like that, with anyone. Rebecca scrolled through the messages from Simone for a while.

"Okay, here it is." She held the phone up for Lana to see the code and type it in, unlocking the mysteries previously trapped in the slim box.

"Actually, I am hungry. I'll take it to my room."

"Now, Simone, you know I don't like you having food in your room. How about eat it at the table? It'll do you good to sit up and be out of that room."

"Never mind. I'll eat later," Lana said. She had other, much more important things to do.

"You really must not feel well. Fine. Just bring the dish back down as soon as you're done." The mother put pancakes and eggs on a large plate and handed it to me with a fork.

"Thanks," Lana said and turned to go back up the stairs.

"You sure you aren't coming down with something, Simone," the mother asked.

"I'll be fine," Lana called back. At least she'd given the woman some attention so she wouldn't be bothered when it mattered.

Rebecca looked back at Lana. Something was different. Perhaps the dreams and nightmares were beginning to wear on Simone. Her daughter seemed a little off this morning. She shook her head. She was eighteen. A lot of things were off at eighteen.

> *I could hardly believe Rebecca brushed it off so quickly. Couldn't she tell this wasn't her daughter? I guess Lana was smart enough to keep the interaction short. I really wanted to scream in that* moment, *'That is not your daughter!' but then what good would that have done when everything she could see told her it was Simone? My hands were still tied.*

Upstairs, Lana closed and quietly locked the door, wanting privacy to investigate her new life. In her hands, she had access to almost every piece of data she could need. She went to the contacts and searched for Locke. Three contacts showed up. There was one with mom, one with dad, and then one unmarked. That must be her sister.

She pulled up Clara, and it was the same girl from the home screen. Lana went back to pull up the contacts marked mom and dad. She found the names Jeffrey and Rebecca. At least now she knew the names of her parents and her sister.

She then opened up the social apps on the phone and scrolled through. She didn't have many friends, but there were all kinds of messages to her about her missing school and a math test. They really did seem like they cared. At least now she had a clue of who she needed to know.

She clicked on Simone's profile information to find out more about her. The phone rang again. It was Taylor. Lana hit ignore and continued to dig for information about her new identity.

Her birthday was November thirtieth. They had the same birthday! She really was only eighteen! She'd hoped what she'd heard from her new sister in the middle of the night hadn't been right. *Geesh. I have to relive three many years again?*" Lana thought.

She went back to see what pages were in her history. Lana Fier's old high school popped up. What were the chances? She'd graduated from there when Simone was a freshman. Lana smiled. It really was such a small world.

She was back in her hometown, but on the other side of the tracks now, where she used to imagine she should have lived if things had been different.

> *Maxwell had better figure this out quickly. His actions are going to make me look bad. A crusader can't afford this type of error. He needs to hurry up and do whatever he is going to do to make all this right again. He is skating on thin* ice, *and that poor* girl, *Simone is caught in the middle.*

"You need to hurry Max. You can't screw with the innocents. We've been over that. Fix it and fast," was the thought I sent to Maxwell as he handled the situation he'd created.

FIFTEEN

Simone

"EXCUSE ME, SIR?" SIMONE said, addressing the old man with gray hair and mustache sitting behind the desk. "Have you seen this man?"

She held up the sketch Taylor had made and hoped the answer was yes.

He stood up slowly and looked at the picture in Simone's hand. His blue and grey security uniform looked freshly starched and pressed though they clung to his protruding stomach.

The name badge sewn onto his shirt read Mr. Jenkins.

"Well, the eyes here are a little kinder, but it looks a lot like the same man who left here, say, about an hour and a half ago. Yeah." Mr. Jenkins held the picture closer as he looked over his glasses and nodded. "That's him alright. What do ya need him for?" he asked peering over the rim of his bifocal glasses at Simone and Taylor now. "And you Taylor, you look like you could do with some sleep."

"I know, Mr. Jenkins. I haven't had time to. Things have been keeping me up at night," she said smiling sweetly.

"Mr. Jenkins, did you happen to catch his name, or where he was going, or what he wanted, or..." Taylor kicked Simone in the leg with her foot where Mr. Jenkins couldn't see. Simone stopped asking questions to glare at her.

"Enough questions, young lady. I don't believe I've ever met you before. Don't come down this way much, do ya?" Mr. Jenkins asked as he put his hands back to find the armrests and sit back down.

"I guess not. Do you know any of those things I asked? His name maybe?" Simone said, unwilling to relent.

"Oh yeah, called himself Maxwell something or other. He was looking for some gal up here in this dorm, but I told him he couldn't go up like that. He was asking for someone named Lena or Lara or..." Mr. Jenkins struggled to remember the name.

"Was it Lana?" Despite being sure of the answer, Simone needed to ask. She needed to hear him say it as confirmation of what she already knew.

"Yes! That's it. How'd you know? Somebody done gone and went and told her, huh? Well, I'll be. News travels fast around here. I tell you that's one thing for sure," he said, smacking the toothpick hanging from his lips.

Simone ignored his speculative comments. It wouldn't do him any good to know that Simone was Lana. At least she was right now.

"What did this guy, Maxwell, say after you told him he couldn't go up? Do you know where he went?" Simone asked.

"You sure ask a lot of questions. Is he in some sort of trouble? Or, are you?"

Mr. Jenkins narrowed his eyes as he looked back and forth between Simone, Taylor, and the drawing still in Simone's hands.

"I'm sorry. I can't tell you if he's in trouble or if he is the trouble. I need to find him, and fast." Simone hoped her elusive answer satisfied the guard.

"Well, let's see. He said he'd be back later. Then he asked if I'd still be here. I don't know what he took me for. A fool or something? Like I haven't heard that one before," Mr. Jenkins chuckled slightly under his breath.

"So, he's coming back, huh? He didn't say when? Just that he'd come back?" Taylor asked, leaning on the desk.

I could see Taylor's wheels turning as she started asking questions. She was a smart girl. Mr. Jenkins shrugged his shoulders as if to say he didn't know.

"Listen, Mr. Jenkins. Don't tell him we were down here asking about him or showed you this picture or anything about this little chat. Okay?

Please?" Taylor asked as she continued to lean on the counter.

"Sure thing. I didn't like him, anyway. Seemed like a shady character to me." He turned back to sit in the chair that squeaked slightly under his weight.

"Thanks, Mr. Jenkins. You are the best," Taylor smiled.

"See you two later and try to get some sleep, young lady. You don't wanna burn yourself out this early in the semester."

"Yes, sir. Bye!"

Mr. Jenkins waved them off before he went back to scrolling through his phone and laughing.

Taylor pulled Simone's arm and pushed her out the door and up the stairs to the dorm room. She flew through their room door, still pulling Simone along. When they finally stopped running, she started jumping up and down in the middle of the room, smiling and giggling.

She grabbed Simone's hands, and Simone couldn't help but jump with her. They had a real clue and a name. Even better, they knew he was coming back. Success. Simone's jumping and excitement ended abruptly as the reality of what had actually taken place began to dawn on her. He was coming back.

Suddenly the room seemed to draw in on her, casting a shadow around her, trying to strangle her. The dusty white blinds hanging from the window were too close; the walls seemed to press against her shoulders and the floor pushed up against her feet. Even the ceiling joined in the action of boxing Simone into a tighter and tighter dark space.

Her head was reeling at what had just taken place. This man, Maxwell, wanted to kill Simone. Her. Lana. Did he even know that he'd screwed up with this mind-body switching thing? They'd been crossed by mistake. She knew from the last dream with him that he'd been convinced that she was Lana. He was so convinced that he'd made it come true.

Lana

Lana Fier paced around her new surroundings, thinking about what could have happened that brought her here. Maxwell had messed up! Maybe Max had thought Simone was Lana because he forgot to look for the present murderer and instead still had the image of Lana from three years earlier.

He'd let his rage and anger in his search for vengeance on the eighteen-year-old girl who'd killed Mickal cloud his judgment and reasoning. For that, Lana was grateful, even if she was confused. How he'd managed to do this was beyond her. Some kind of magician? Dark magician? She'd never believed in that kind of thing, but looking at herself in the mirror, she was ready to believe anything.

He was still looking for that high school student rather than the woman she now was. Lana smiled to herself and then at the reflection in the mirror.

She pulled the dark hair back from her face. She did bear a slight resemblance to Simone, but aside from the same birthday, Simone being the age Lana was when it happened, and the same high school, Lana didn't see much else they had in common.

"He probably let his temper cloud his judgment, like Mickal had," she thought with a laugh.

> *I wanted to slap the silly smile off her lips and send her back myself.* Lana's reflection in the mirror was still foreign as she let herself wonder about the dreams she'd had a few weeks before. Dreams that had scared her awake, sweating, near tears, and sometimes crying out for help.

They'd woken up Taylor too, and had her dorm-mate Kathy running into the room on more than one occasion. Maybe Maxwell had hit the right wavelength, then lost it. Surely, he had to know what he'd done. The mistake was too big. If he didn't know, then Simone Locke could deal with him and she'd be free.

Lana tried to push it out of her mind. She didn't want to think about him or why she was there anymore. It wasn't her problem as long as she kept Simone away. She hoped Maxwell found Simone in the body she'd occupied for twenty-one years and made it permanent.

It never should've been her problem, anyway. She'd never asked for the life she'd been dished out. But that nosy brother Maxwell had to go probing into everyone's business.

She thought about Mickal. Would she have said yes if she were older? She knew she would only be lying to herself if she even tried to think the answer might be yes. Each time she saw that future, she saw her own parents' miserable, disastrous lives. Never would that be her. Mickal wouldn't have made her or anyone a good husband.

Between his temper and mean streak, he would've hurt whoever he was with, either physically or emotionally. Most likely both. She comforted herself with the notion that she had most likely done the world a favor. Saved some woman down the road from whatever damage and destruction would've come out of one of his tantrums.

She'd seen firsthand that day by the lake what his fury looked and felt like. She shivered for a moment but quickly pushed it aside. That was a long time ago. She'd moved on and was doing fine.

And now with this brand new second chance at a good life, she was doing even better. She would do it the same way if she ever had to go back. After the initial shock had worn off years before, there had never been any regret.

SIXTEEN

Simone

SIMONE PLOPPED ONTO THE faded caramel-colored carpet to think while Taylor stared at her. He was coming back. He was coming back to get her, Lana. She could hardly breathe. Maybe she would come out and ask him to give them their bodies back; after all, it was Lana he wanted, not Simone. But what if he refused? Anyone who could do this couldn't be stable.

He could be a raving lunatic, and then there'd be no rationalization. But he wouldn't refuse. He would have to switch them because he wanted revenge on Lana Fier, not some girl accidentally living in her body.

Simone would wait for him to come back to the dorm office. Mr. Jenkins would send a text to Taylor, whenever that was. She had no idea when that might be, but no matter how long, she would wait.

"So you really are going to wait on that Maxwell guy to show back up?" Taylor asked. Simone hadn't noticed her standing there until that moment.

"Mmmhmm. I have to. I hope it's soon." Simone's tremors were noticeable as she got up to look out the window.

From where she was on the fourth floor, she had a straight and unobstructed view of the parking lot, which now had fewer cars. The day was winding down and commuter students were heading home like those people working in the high rises.

Simone pulled the blinds so they'd slant down towards the parking lot. There was no need to give herself and her room away unnecessarily. She was sure he'd be looking at the windows.

> *I know I would have, and I knew him well enough to know her instincts were right.*

Simone watched through the slats for the gray sports sedan while sitting crouched on the floor. Her stomach growled and groaned beneath the purple shirt.

She hadn't eaten anything all day, and the only sign of her physical neglect was her stomach talking. She placed a hand instinctively across her stomach, but she still couldn't eat. Her appetite had gone with her identity. When Simone had her own body back, maybe then she could think about eating. Until then she was only willing to hold on to a sliver of 'give a care' she had for Lana. Lana Evilyn Fier.

Simone glanced over at Taylor, who was busy doing an online search for the name Maxwell in the city of Atlanta. She'd never find it. The city was too big, and they only had one name. They didn't even know if it was a first name or a last name. But Taylor was still typing away and scrolling. Simone would be forever indebted to her. Even if successfully getting back to her body meant not being able to repay her.

"Taylor, thank you for helping me and, most of all, for believing me. I was so lost. I still feel lost, but I didn't have any idea what to do. If you ever need anything, I'm here for you."

"Hey now, don't go getting all mushy on me. You act like I saved your life or something. But you're welcome just the same," Taylor said, shooting Simone the same smile she'd given Mr. Jenkins. She turned back and started scrolling again.

The hour that passed moved at the pace of days in the anxious dorm room where Simone sat with Taylor, staring out of the window. "When was he coming?" she thought nervously.

"I can't take this anymore. Come on. Let's wait downstairs where we can be there as soon as he shows up here," Taylor said.

"You think that's a good idea, Taylor? To already be down there? We can see him coming from up here," Simone questioned with obvious hesitation.

"Sure, why not? What's he gonna do? No! Better question is what are you gonna do? You're the one caught in the middle of this mess. What are you going to do get out of it?"

Taylor had a point, and suddenly Simone's plan of asking the man who wanted her dead for a switch back seemed rather pathetic, but she told her anyway. What else did she have to lose?

"I'm going to ask him to switch our minds back. I think he will because he wants revenge on Lana, not me. He has nothing against me. I don't think he does, at least." Simone's hands shook even as she said it. She couldn't escape the feeling that her life might end soon.

"He 'shouldn't have anything against you at least, you mean," Taylor clarified.

Simone looked down through the window one more time. She hoped she hadn't missed something. They walked out the door and this time closed it behind them as they continued in uncomfortable silence down the stairs and to the dorm office. Simone hoped Mr. Jenkins was still there.

Seventeen

Simone

Downstairs in the lobby, the uncomfortable and unusual silence continued. There was no sign of Mr. Jenkins. No sound of him somewhere in a backroom laughing to himself. Simone and Taylor sat on the equally uncomfortable plastic waiting chairs in anticipation of Maxwell's entrance.

Twenty-five minutes passed before they noticed a man dressed in a black suit and a black wool fedora hat approaching the office doors.

The gait was unmistakable. The tinted windows kept him from seeing them as they sat frozen. Mr. Jenkins still hadn't come back.

"What should we do?" Taylor whispered to Simone as he got nearer.

"Let's get behind the desk."

Taylor got up and Simone followed her as they scooted across the lobby to the security desk and found their way under the large desk. The door creaked as it opened, and the heavy sound of boots echoed on the white tile floors. In what seemed like three giant steps, he was at the desk. There was silence.

Simone couldn't hear him breathing or moving. Her heart thumped against her hands as she pressed her body tight into the back of the desk. A moment later, the sound of a loud and shrill 'ding' rang out from the bell that sat on the security desk, startling her. Simone's head bumped against the top of the desk as she jumped.

Taylor glared at Simone as they both curled up tighter. Simone's eyes filled with fear as she silently hoped he hadn't heard the thud.

But there was no such luck. In moments, the long strides were coming around the desk.

"Oh. Hey there. I see you made your way back. You here to try and see that girl again, right?" It was Mr. Jenkins coming from a back room.

"Where the heck had he been all this time?" Simone wondered. The footsteps stopped and turned back around.

"Is there anyone else in here with you? I thought I heard something." Maxwell searched behind Mr. Jenkins as he sat in his chair.

"No. Don't think so. These old buildings can creak and moan sometimes, like they have a life of their own, if you know what I mean." Mr. Jenkins leaned back a bit.

There was no way he could miss seeing Simone's foot from under the desk. He peered over his glasses at Maxwell. "You can have a seat over there if you want to."

Simone's legs shook under the desk as she tried to control her nerves, but there was nothing she could do. Her plan hadn't been very well thought out. She was just a high school kid; she reminded herself. She'd never needed to prepare for something like this. She closed her eyes and tried to calm her breathing, but the tapping of Maxwell's fingers on the wooden desk reminded her of how close to danger they were.

The only thing between her and Maxwell was Mr. Jenkins, who looked like he'd had this same post since Simone's mother was in college. Shaking that rattled Simone's entire body eventually rattled the desk. Taylor tried to hold Simone still, but it was pointless.

"What's under there!? Maxwell's big black boots clapped the floor full force as he stormed behind the desk.

He pushed Mr. Jenkins chair back, exposing Simone's quivering foot. He reached his large hand down, grabbing her sneaker with his long, bony fingers. He dragged her out by the white tennis shoes as he reached back and slammed Mr. Jenkins' chair against the wall, making him fall out in pain.

He was strong, and his anger seemed to only make him stronger. Taylor tried to crawl out from under the desk and make a dash back around, but Maxwell's powerful arms grabbed hold of her leg, keeping her down on the floor.

Trapped between the desk and the wall, they had nowhere to go. Maxwell pulled Mr. Jenkins up, hurt and limping, and pushed him into the closet, slamming the door. He jammed one of the sitting chairs against it as Simone searched the scarcely supplied security desk for a weapon.

The only things on the desk were a monitor, a small stack of paper forms, a cup of pens, and the small bell which was out of reach. Simone quickly grabbed a pen and ran up behind Maxwell. It was their only chance.

He turned and took hold of her hand, twisting it until the pen fell clanging to the tile floor near their feet. She raised her foot to kick him, but it had barely left the floor before she was in a chokehold, kicking and lashing at him. But it did no good, as he threw her, into the lobby chair.

"Don't try it again!" he shouted at Simone, his eyes wild and his pupils dilated. "And you, I have no business with you."

He grabbed Taylor by the neck and opened the closet door, tossing her in beside Mr. Jenkins. He was hunched on the floor, leaning against the wall, holding his head, blood dripping down his brow.

"He's hurt," Taylor pleaded. "He needs help."

"You can get him help as soon as I'm done here."

Maxwell slammed the door again to Taylor's yells of "NO!" and jammed the chair against it again. Taylor banged on the door loudly and cried out from behind the closed door.

EIGHTEEN

Simone

"SO YOU ARE HERE," Maxwell spoke harshly and in a deep mellow voice.

He slowly turned his long body until he faced her. As he came closer, Simone could smell the whiskey, hot on his breath. The icy gaze of his eyes seemed to reflect back her fear. They were in a deadlock with hers.

"Yes. I'm here. But I'm not who you think I am," Simone said, not moving her eyes but unable to hide the quiver in her voice.

"You are exactly who I think you are." He sounded as if he were trying to convince himself as much as he was her.

"No, I'm not. I just have to tell you one thing, Mr. Maxwell. You messed up. I am not Lana Fier. My name is Simone Locke and I want my body back."

Simone's voice and body seemed to relax some, despite the fear and her quivering. She'd stated it plainly and aloud. She was still breathing. From the white molded plastic chair, she searched for the strength she had to convince herself existed.

"I want my body back right now because I don't want Lana's life and it's not fair that you did this to me and want me to pay for her mistakes and your mistakes!" Simone was now almost yelling.

Her voice shook less than it had been, and her body had stopped trembling. Simone was getting her courage back. As she felt herself growing stronger, that courage was accompanied by a healthy dose of rage that put fire in her eyes.

He was going to change her back, and after that Lana could deal with her own life and her own problems. Hopefully not by being killed by this psycho, but if she were guilty, then justice should be served.

Simone wanted to think the best and hope the best, but the possible murderer had more than willingly thrown her under the bus being driven by Maxwell, the maniac.

Maxwell paused, and his expression changed. He was angry, but it was different. Simone watched, wondering what he was going to do.

"I WANT LANA FIER!!!" he roared, causing Simone to sit back, her head now against the royal blue wall.

> *I drew closer, hidden even from Maxwell. The veins in his neck bulged with blood as he said each* word, *and his face turned the shade of crimson red. He didn't want some other girl in Lana's body. He wanted Lana, the girl who had killed Mickal three years*

ago. Maxwell needed to get Lana Fier.
I hoped he would end this now.

"If this really wasn't Lana, where was she hiding?" Maxwell asked himself.

Simone sat with her eyes closed, asking quietly for help. She could feel his steely eyes boring into her own, wondering if she was telling the truth. Her eyes were sealed as she waited for the prayer to reach heaven or whoever would hear it.

In her hand she still held the pen.

"I'm on assignment already. They aren't going to listen to your plea for help," he mocked. "Tell me where Lana Fier is, or be ready to be served her justice for her crime."

The idea of him killing her, in my body, sent me reeling. I stood up from the chair. "No. Whatever assignment you think you're on, you're wrong. And I'm not going to help you kill someone else."

"Fine. Then accept the justice I would've given her," he growled.

This was it. It had gone too far. Maxwell was willing to knowingly hurt an innocent due to his anger. Now I would be allowed to step in. Between her request for help and Maxwell's escalation, Raguel could not tell me I'd overstepped.

Simone pulled her hand back, this time dropping low, out of his immediate reach, and jabbed the pen into his stomach. He yelled out in pain, falling back onto the desk. "You'll pay for sure now. I don't care who you are."

As he lunged toward her, blinded by rage, I reclaimed the project. "Not today, Maxwell."

For moments that seemed to stretch on infinitely Simone heard nothing in the room besides her thoughts. He was speaking, but it became background noise, like the banging and yells coming from the closet.

Simone's eyelids clouded over as the light in the room no longer reflected on the inside of her lids. The sound of powerful thunder shook her seat. She jumped, startled by the sound.

Nineteen

Simone

From the soft, plush carpet of her bedroom floor, Simone seemed to float to the bed. She was surprised at the softness beneath her. Gone was the hard, cool plastic chair. Simone blinked her eyes again and looked around. It was her room.

Her real room.

Familiar.

Her things surrounded her.

The sense of home rushed back into Simone. Her knowledge of her self-identity penetrated deeply through her entire being as she reconnected with her body. Simone was back. She was no longer Lana Fier, and she could now be herself and in her own life.

She stood up cautiously, to look at her reflection in the mirror. As her eyes met the face she'd always known, a sense of relief came over her. She really was back. It was her body she saw, her hands, her face.

Simone wondered what awaited Lana. Her secrets were exposed. Her roommate, Taylor, knew the truth. Maxwell knew where to find her. He might have already gotten Lana. Either way, she wouldn't be able to escape and would have to deal with whatever happened when she was Simone's age.

Despite hoping Lana would do it the right way, with sadness she knew, from her brief glimpse into who Lana Fier was, Lana would choose otherwise. But that was there, not here. And Simone was here.

She was home! Her part of the ordeal was over. Then she thought of Taylor who'd helped her through the ordeal and how she was back in the dorm with the girl who was willing to let Simone die to keep her secret. Or was Taylor still in the closet with that maniac on the outside!?, she thought.

Simone was home, but she still wasn't done. She found her phone near the pillow on the bed and scrolled through a dozen missed calls from friends to find Taylor's number and call her back. After a few rings, a scared voice answered in a hushed whisper.

"Hello?"

"Taylor. It's me. It's Simone Locke. I'm back in my body. I'm calling the cops to come to the dorm. Just hold on. I'm going to use three-way, so don't hang up. It's going to be okay."

"Thank you. I called, but they couldn't hear me or get my location. Can't talk," said Taylor, who stopped speaking so Maxwell wouldn't come in.

As Simone waited on the line with Taylor, she heard the sirens in the background. Moments later, Simone heard Maxwell yell, "She killed him. She killed my brother!"

Taylor was again banging on the closet door. Simone could hear the clanging of the chair being moved and then the screeching of the closet door opening.

"She did kill his brother. I don't know what happened, but she did. But I believe this man came here to get her. Mr. Jenkins needs help. All I want is out of here."

Simone heard her strong new friend Taylor break down as an officer led her away from the madness. The phone went silent.

The plush beanbag chair looked inviting. It had always been her favorite place to sit in her room. She let herself sink into it so she could take it all in. After a moment of letting the malleable chair mold to her, a crawling sensation overcame Simone. She shot up from the chair.

Lana Fier had been here. In this room. With her things.

It felt tainted, like Lana's residue was left all over everything. But this was Simone's life, and she intended to keep it.

Simone felt the carpet, her carpet, under her bare feet. She opened the bedroom door and stuck her head out. “I’m back!” she yelled out the door, and her voice echoed through the house, reverberating off the walls.

“Where’d you go?” Rebecca yelled upstairs with confusion.

Simone quickly thought about all that had happened. Lana hadn’t gone to school that day, and Simone was still in the orange pajamas she’d put on the night before. Her mom had no idea what had taken place.

“Nowhere. I guess I must’ve been dreaming.”

“Well, make sure you bring the plate down you used this morning. Remember that was a one-time thing.

“Okay,” she called back. She’d gladly take it down and was completely alright with it being a one-time thing. Never again did she want to experience anything like that.

TWENTY

THIS ASSIGNMENT MEANS MORE work is required. A great deal more work. I'm pissed and have little patience for it right now. I hate having my hands tied until they decide it's okay for me to act.

Maxwell almost blew it. He'd gotten lost in the act of seeking vengeance and overused his powers, almost causing an innocent to be harmed.

I'm glad Lana has been brought to justice, but his single-minded, dogged determination in first balancing the act that took his brother was neither balanced nor just.

He'd seen what happened that day, yet refused to see his brother's role in it. He refuses to see how losing control of his faculties causes him to lose control of his power. It makes him a liability. If he is to be the yang to my yin, a great deal of work has to be done. Working with humans is always precarious. That's what I told Raguel any chance I could. It was especially so with anyone who's already got a hot temper.

I've existed in the shadows doing this work for longer than I can remember. It's an endless dance of loneliness, existing between the great expanse of the universe and the limitations of Earth. I am quite accustomed to collapsing my energy into human form, dense and clumsy, so I can amongst these beings. Not a bad thing, just a reality. I have enjoyed many human experiences.

I watch now and smirk as Simone Locke is able to resume her life. He'd forced me to step in and save her because he was too stubborn to or unable. I am not quite sure which one yet. I'll find out though when we debrief.

Unlike my sister, I am assigned the more difficult side of karma. I don't get to dole out blessings and good fortune. All the stuff people go thanking God for. Instead, I am charged with correcting and balancing the wrongs committed – in thought and action.

He'd seen what happened that day, yet refused to see his brother's role in it. He refuses to see how losing control of his faculties causes him to lose control of his power. It makes him a liability. If he is to be the yang to my yin, a great deal of work has to be done. Working with humans is always precarious. That's what I told Raguel any chance I could. It was especially so with anyone who's already got a hot temper.

I've existed in the shadows doing this work for longer than I can remember. It's an endless dance of loneliness, existing between the great expanse of the universe and the limitations of Earth. I am quite accustomed to collapsing my energy into human form, dense and clumsy, so I can amongst these beings. Not a bad thing, just a reality. I have enjoyed many human experiences.

Why choose to collapse into the form I have? So I can experience life in a way most don't. I get to see the authentic truth of people. But the job doesn't care that I enjoy the humanness of it, it demands that I create balance.

I watch now and smirk as Simone Locke is able to resume her life. He'd forced me to step in and save her because he was too stubborn or unable. I am not quite sure which one yet. I'll find out though when we debrief.

Unlike my sister, I am assigned the more difficult side of karma. I don't get to dole out blessings and good fortune. All the stuff people go thanking God for. Instead, I am charged with correcting and balancing the wrongs committed. That alone will keep us busy for lifetimes.

And then people want to call me a b%^*h or the devil. Either way, they bring it on themselves. They can call it whatever they want, but it's all the same force.

There is a cost that comes with the power I hold. I am stuck between lower heaven and the base of Earth's humanity. I see the dark and grimy side of humans. I am so close to it, covered in the energetic muck that I can only ascend so high before being stopped because of the darkness that constantly surrounds me. It isn't fair.

Every case I handle leaves another layer of spiritual grime on my soul, tethering me further to the Earth's base. I don't just need the help, I need them to act as conduits that keep me from being completely buried by the weight of these assignments. And working with someone like Maxwell only makes it worse.

What did I do to deserve this twisted fate? I am an administrator of justice, and yet my own existence at times feels unjust. But I have my duty and my honor. I answer to a higher power, and there are things that simply must be done.

Don't get me wrong, it's not all bad. Seeing the guilty pay is rewarding. Being trapped in the middle, isn't. But, if I can't keep my energy clean, I must ensure that at least the work is done without pulling me further into the abyss.

And, I had time on my side. Time to develop better crusaders. If the Universal Karmic Force wouldn't give me the reward I need, I would build a system that's better, make us undeniable. What I'm building keeps them clear, me clear, and gives me a path to a different kind of justice.

When Raguel assigned Maxwell to me, it was with special status as a hybrid human. His father was mortal. Very mortal and his mother had been like me. Mickal shared the same father, but his mother was of Earth as well. Maxwell's wreckage, from the police reports and bruised egos to the collateral damage, serves as a permanent contrast to the focused and intentional balancing I expect from anyone on my team.

I suppose Maxwell being a hybrid is why Raguel thought he would fit this role well, being able to walk in both worlds. But there seems to be more of his father in him than his mother.

I heard Raguel's argument, and I'd seen that he'd proven himself strong, focused, and committed to the long process of administering justice. I also saw his temper, irrationality, addictive personality, and stubbornness. Maxwell proved that being a hybrid doesn't grant you wisdom; it only grants you more capacity to wreak havoc when you lose your temper. I am done with that volatility. To his credit, he was tenacious, and sometimes it can take time for plans to line up and for karma to be balanced.

In the meantime, only heaven can take him out. Neither of us is subject to the regular forces of humanity's physical laws. But neither of us can escape the laws that order the universe, whether we like it or not.

The café close to the University downtown is one of my favorite coffee spots. The people coming and going include all types - a microcosm of humanity in a city that gives me plenty to stay busy. The lattes are always perfectly steamed without scalding my tongue and the baristas actually smile. I'll enjoy one while I think about the other smaller assignments on my plate.

I know Raguel will be coming soon with another assignment for me to fit in and to continue the training with Maxwell. It seems there is always work to be done. The next round won't be like this one. Maxwell will watch and learn as I handle the next assignment.

Maxwell, yes Maxwell. I suppose I should go get him and bring him back here with me. He forgets I have the power to dial back his abilities and right now he's stuck. Waiting in the police precinct should help sober him up. He needs a little dose of karma himself.

I laugh, almost losing my mouthful of coffee. He's six and half feet tall, but I can bring him to his knees. On second thought, maybe I'll let him sweat it out for a while longer.

***

I hope you enjoyed reading **Crossed**. *Would you* ***please leave a brief review*** *to help others find it? Word of mouth is one of the best ways for an author's works to be discovered and it won't take but a minute.*

Thank you so much and I hope you enjoy my other works. The free short story, The Wait, is included.

ALSO BY BERNETTE

Fiction

Curse of the Woods (Fairytale Fantasy)
Crossed (Urban Fantasy)
Haven to Hold (Cozy Light Fantasy)
Light of the Dark Moon (Epic Fantasy)
Star Jumpers (Science-Fantasy)
The Story of Ervin James (Historical Fiction)

Self-Help and Poetry

The 1-Thing Way
Love Me Journal of Haikus (Poetry)
Manifest Money in a Month
Money Skills for Your Rich Life
Pendulums and Protection
Protect and Clear with the Divine (Self-Help)
Reclaim Your Body for Life
Resist Persist (Poetry)
Success is in Your Story

Find these books and more: *BernetteSherman.com*

About the Author

About the Author

Bernette Sherman is a multi-genre author of cozy fantasy, sci-fantasy, fantasy, poetry, plays, and self-help. She's a wife, mom, and coffee-drinker who enjoys and supports the performing arts. Learn more about Bernette and find her books and social media at BernetteSherman.com.

Website: BernetteSherman.com
My Books: BernetteSherman.com/books-by-bernette
Instagram, YouTube, and TikTok: @IAmBernette
Tiktok: @BernetteWrites
Facebook @IAmBernetteSherman

ABOUT THE AUTHOR

BERNETTE IS A MULTI-GENRE writer and creative with a passion for creating and inspiring positive change in people. She lives in the metro Atlanta area with her family.

Website:BernetteSherman.com
Tiktok: Tiktok.com/@bernettewrites
Instagram:
Facebook: .
Books:

The Wait (Chapter One)

(BONUS SHORT STORY)

One

Whether rain, shine, or even the cold winds that brought glistening white snow and frozen waters; I would see him. Every day, he'd be there, sitting in that same spot, waiting. Waiting as the commuters made their way to work. Waiting as they came and had lunch around the pier. Waiting as they made their way back past him again, on their somber journeys home. Then, when the sun was gone, so was he.

What he was waiting for all this time, I didn't know. From the window where I watched the world, I chronicled his comings and goings in my mind. I never saw him arrive and never saw him walk away, but each day he was the same, never bringing anything with him besides himself and never leaving anything behind.

I opened the window to let in the autumn air. September struggled to hang on to its languishing summer, taking shelter in the leaves of the trees that still clung to the branches. Nevertheless, they would have to fall soon. And, eventually, winter would come.

I breathed in the dryness of the breeze, sneezing as it tickled my nostrils. Today would be the day. I would finally leave my perfect fifth-story bedroom view in my oversized townhouse and walk down the stairs and out the front door.

"I can do it," I whispered in repetition to myself.

It had been two years since I'd crossed the threshold of my doorstep, but today I would do more than reach out for my packages and mail.

He was waiting for me. He didn't know it, but I had to go to that bench and sit with him. I looked out the window once more, trying to gather my courage. I'd showered that morning and for the first time since Labor Day, I finally shaved my scraggly beard and mustache.

He might think I'm strange. He might get up and walk away. Who did I think I was? I would be invading his space. What if he was waiting on someone and today was the day they came? What if my being there scared them away? Doubt wracked my mind as I wrestled with my own insecurities and fears.

I paced back and forth in front of my bed, my hands clasped behind my damp hair. I was foolish to think this man would want to have anything to do with me. He'd been fine, sitting there day after day for at least as long as I'd been sitting in my home. Thinking back, I'd lost track of time and no longer knew exactly how long it had been.

I shuffled back to the window, trying to regain the little courage I'd summoned. The fresh air felt good. It smelled good. It felt inviting as it wafted into my room, carrying with it the hints of aged flowers and leaves. He was still there. His brown hat leaning to the side. His eyes seemed to glance at every person walking by; just long enough to realize that no one passing was the one he was looking for.

My gaze fell on my reflection in the dusty mirror. I hadn't seen myself fully dressed in more than two years. Time rushed back to me as I saw myself in my humble humanness. It was two years ago this month that I'd last been out. My last exit from my home marked by the funeral. After trying on three pairs of pants with zippers and buttons, I realized my clothes no longer fit me. Sweatpants and a large sweatshirt would have to suffice.

"I'm going out, Molly."

She smiled from her seat in the blue wing-back chair. Her white dress accented her olive skin. I kissed her as I headed downstairs. The door loomed ahead of me. As I got closer, my head began to swim, and I swayed as if intoxicated. The churning of my stomach made me turn for the restroom, grateful for the momentary excuse. After dry heaving over the toilet for several minutes, I stood up and weakly took a mouthful of water.

"I'm really going this time," I yelled back up again to Molly.

I knew she was already looking out the window to see if I'd done it. I closed my eyes and pulled the door open. The air hit me, nearly taking the wind out of me. It had been months since I'd even stood in the doorway long enough to feel it. I went to take a step out, but my legs didn't move and my feet wouldn't budge. I felt a gentle touch on my back and knew it was okay. I slowly picked up one leg, forcing it down, and then dragged the other. Once on my front step, I took a deep breath and closed the door. I was outside and now only had to make it down the steps and around to the pier.

My legs were lead cannonballs as I took the three steps down to the sidewalk. Lightheaded, my heart was racing so hard I thought I might faint. No one seemed to notice except me.

"I can do this." My steps were slow and pained, but I was moving towards the man on the bench. From my bedroom window the pier had seemed so close, but the walk now felt like miles.

I looked back at the house to see the window that had been my main view to the world for too long. Molly smiled at me. I know she must've been proud. I would do this for her.

Two

I FIDGETED WITH THE single house key in my hand as I walked around the buildings between my townhouse and his bench. My hands shook as I got nearer to his bench. I eased myself as casually as I could onto the other end, trying not to cause any obvious disturbance. He turned his head slightly, taking me in. I nodded at him, and with a slight look of surprise, he returned the nod.

"Good morning," I said with a nervous smile and taking the chance to speak.

"Good morning," he returned, politely.

"Beautiful fall day, isn't it?" I had become rusty in my small talk, but I didn't care.

"It certainly is. A good day to get out." He continued to look at those passing by.

"Are you waiting on someone?" I had to ask.

"Yes. I'm waiting. I said I'd be right here; so here I am." He smiled with a slight blush that seemed to be filled with expectation.

"Have you been waiting long?" I needed to know.

"Oh no. I just got here this morning. She'll be here soon."

Now I was confused.

"I mean, have you been waiting long for the day she's coming?" I tried to ask more clearly.

"No. I'll be meeting her here today. Just like we planned." This time his answer was accompanied by an assured smile.

I studied his suit and jacket. He was dressed so much better than I was that I almost felt ashamed. He didn't seem to notice, though. He was much more fashionable and put together than I had ever been, even before the funeral.

We sat in silence for a while. I was unsure of what to say next. I had no real plan for coming down to the bench, and the only thing I'd brought was a single key.

He looked at me curiously for a moment. "What brings you here? Are you waiting for someone too?"

"Me? No, I just came out for some fresh air. I don't usually get out much." It was the lame truth. "I don't live but a couple blocks from here, over in one of the townhouse buildings."

"Maybe you'll get to see her. She lives in one of those townhouses a few blocks away too. She's a real beauty." The smile crossing his face made me nostalgic in a way he could never understand.

The stranger turned to me and leaned in slightly. When he spoke this time, it was in a hushed voice as if it were a secret. "Today's the day. I'm going to ask her to leave him and come with me. I'm going to take her on a long drive out of the city, and that's when I'm going to do it. I want her to leave all this and come away with me." A wistful look filled his eyes, and he stared somewhere into the distance. "Hmmm. That's the first time I said it aloud. I hope I can say it again when it counts, with her." A chuckle escaped as his fingers fidgeted with the brim of the hat resting on his knee.

"Hopefully she'll say yes and not break the other poor sucker's heart too much," I joked back. He laughed as his eyes did the usual scan of the folks walking by.

"How long are you waiting out here for her?" I asked after sitting in silence for several more minutes. I was beginning to feel anxious. I hadn't been outside for that long in more than two years and all of the air was beginning to get to me.

"You feeling okay? You look a little…ill." He slid to the edge of the bench, as far away from me as possible without getting up. I was silently hoping I wouldn't go into the dry heaves again. Up until then, I thought I was doing fine.

"Yeah, just a little light-headed. That's what staying cooped up in the house will do for you." I tried to hide my awkwardness with what sounded like nervous laugh. So much for trying to make light of myself.

“I wouldn’t know. I believe in the outdoors and fresh air. It’s why we chose this place to meet,” he smiled. “The water, the breeze, the people going by. I love it.”

“Hopefully, she’ll come soon. I’ve got to go myself, but maybe I’ll see you around. Good luck.” I was feeling weak and needed to get home and back to Molly. I had done more today than any day so far since I’d started therapy.

“Alright. Maybe next time you see me, I’ll have her with me.” He nodded and waved good-bye.

THREE

I WALKED THROUGH THE door and put the key down. Resting a moment against the closed door, I finally caught what was left of my shallow breath. I didn't understand why he would sit there and lie to me, a stranger. I was sure he didn't really care what I thought. To say that was his only time coming was a flat out lie.

Even barely back in the door, I already knew I would have to go back tomorrow. Molly would be happy I was getting out again. It didn't really matter what happened with him. My getting out of the house was a good start.

The next morning I put on the same sweatpants and a different sweatshirt. I needed to go shopping online soon for clothes that fit and maybe use the treadmill in the spare bedroom. For now, the sweats would have to do. I stole a look out of the window. In the distance, I saw him already sitting on the bench in the same spot. Like all the days before, he sat with his hat resting on his right knee, watching people go by.

This time, I didn't panic as I reached the front door. I grabbed the key and took a deep breath before opening the door and yelling back, "I'm going out again. I'll be back soon."

I walked the couple of blocks around the corner and towards the pier much more quickly this time, pressing my anxiety down each time it tried to slow me from my goal. The lead cannonballs that had been around my ankles yesterday only felt like kid-sized bowling balls. I approached the bench and sat as I'd done the day before. He turned his head slightly and looked at me with a slight nod.

"Hey. How are you?" I asked cautiously.

"Fine. Thank you."

"Beautiful day, isn't it?" I asked, trying to casually strike up a conversation again.

"Yes, it is. A good day to get out." He glanced a little longer at one woman passing by.

"Is it okay if I sit here? You waiting on anyone?"

"I am waiting on someone, but you can sit. Hopefully, she'll be here soon." He sounded optimistic, as if she hadn't stood him up already.

"Oh. That's good. Never give up. Right?" He gave me a confused look as he stole another glance at a woman with dark hair.

"Have you been waiting long?" I was even more confused, and now I could add irritation to confusion. He had the nerve to pretend he didn't remember me. I wasn't remarkable, but I didn't think I was that forgettable, unless he suffered from memory loss. That might explain his answers the day before.

"No, just got here not that long before you showed up." He leaned slightly in my direction with a smile on his face. "I told her I'd meet her right here, so here I am."

"Is it a special day or something? You're dressed up," I said with a gesture at his suit.

As if I'd said something odd, he looked down at himself. A look of confusion crossed his face. "This isn't right. I could swear I put on my khaki pants with a blue button-down shirt. She loves me in blue. We're going on a drive along the river, and why would I wear a suit for that?" he asked as if I held the answer.

"I don't know. I figured you dressed up for her." I mirrored his state of confusion.

"No, I got up and put on my khakis and button-down shirt. I am certain of that. I came down here and she...," his voice trailed off as if suddenly remembering some distant memory that he'd locked away. A look of shock entered his eyes.

"What is it? Are you okay?" I asked.

"She met me right here. She met me, and we walked back to the car. We drove out of the city, just as I'd planned. We drove down along the river where the road curves to follow it. I stopped the car near the bend where there are benches and an open area to sit, and we got out.

She looked like an angel in her white summer dress. We sat down by the lake and I told her."

The man shook his head as if trying to clear his head or shake something away.

FOUR

HE LOOKED BACK TOWARDS me, but he wasn't looking at me. He was somewhere else.

"I told her I wanted to be with her. I told her I wanted to marry her and for us to get away from all of this and our past. We could start again, brand new."

"Well, that's great, right?" I asked, unsure where he was going and why he was there.

"She kept nodding slowly as if she were really listening and considering what I was saying. We had the area to ourselves. It was just the two of us and I was giving her all my love," he looked off towards the water and rose to his feet.

"You went for it, like you said," I smiled at him.

He looked back at me, confused, before he continued speaking. "She stood up and told me she didn't want to leave him and that she needed to end it. She said she planned to marry him. That's what she told me. Then she had the nerve to say she was sorry. We were by the water. We were right by the river, and she said she didn't want me. She wanted him. That loser who she had to drag out the house anytime she wanted to have fun. I was so mad. I mean, she just got me so mad. Something snapped. I'd given everything up already, for her. I...I...all I remember was her lying in the river. She wasn't breathing. She wasn't moving. She wouldn't wake up."

His speech became trance-like. He'd forgotten that I was even there.

"I ran to my car and got in. I sped off. The gas pedal was pressed to the floor, and I wasn't paying attention, and there was an eighteen-wheeler...I swerved and-," his voice faded again as he looked down at himself and touched his suit. "What happened? What happened? Oh no!"

I could see something dawning in his eyes as I let him continue. "I killed her. I killed her. I killed my Molly. And this suit is not what I put on to meet her."

Before I could say anything through my shock at his strange confession, he began backing away from the bench. The lunch crowds descended on the pier for one of the last nice days of early fall. I shook my head, trying to make sense of what he said. I clutched at my chest as my heart began to race again. I couldn't see him. How did I lose him that quickly? The crowd wasn't that thick. What was it he said? "I killed Molly. I killed Molly."

His words echoed in my head. I looked back at where he'd been just moments before, at the space filled with a young man eating a sandwich out of a paper bag. With a surge of energy, I ran the two blocks home, bursting through the door.

"Molly! Molly!"

I ran upstairs to where I'd left her sitting near me in the bedroom. Her blue chair was empty. She was nowhere in our townhouse. She was gone.

***

I hope you enjoyed reading **The Wait**. *Would you* ***please leave a brief review*** *to help others find it? Word of mouth is one of the best ways for an author's works to be discovered and it won't take but a minute.*

www.ingramcontent.com/pod-product-compliance
Lightning Source LLC
LaVergne TN
LVHW050956080826
845145LV00009B/2319